SPURRED
Studs in Spurs

Cat Johnson

Copyright © 2017 Cat Johnson

All rights reserved.

ISBN-13: 978-1546336884
ISBN-10: 1546336885

DEDICATION

As with most things, the creation of a book is not a one-person job. This book is dedicated to all those who helped bring it to life.

STUDS IN SPURS

Unridden
Bucked
Ride
Hooked
Flanked
Thrown
Champion
Spurred
Wrecked

CHAPTER ONE

"Jordan!"

At the sound of his name being shouted, Aaron Jordan stopped halfway across the empty arena. He turned to see Tom Parsons lift an arm and wave him over.

Frowning, Aaron headed across the dirt toward the man, unsure and a little concerned about why the president of the bull-riding association would want to talk to him. It felt a little like being unexpectedly called to the principal's office in high school—not good.

With every step he took, Aaron turned over possible reasons for the summons in his mind. He and the guys had been out at a bar drinking last night, but nothing wild had happened.

Hell, he hadn't even scored with the girl he'd been chatting up.

Of course, the last event had been a different story. Aaron had had his own hotel room for that event rather than sharing with any of the other riders like he was this week. He had taken complete advantage of the privacy.

Crap. Was he in trouble for that night?

Reaching his destination, he couldn't ponder the

circumstances any longer. For better or worse, he'd know soon enough.

"Yes, sir?" In his oldest pair of cowboy boots—the ones with a hole in the sole—Aaron tried not to feel inferior standing opposite this polished man. He'd get around to throwing the boots out one day, but damned if they weren't his most comfortable pair. It was only a small hole.

"I need you to do something for me."

What would Tom Parsons, in his business suit, shiny dress shoes and perfectly cut and combed hair need from him?

"Uh, all right. What d'you need?" Aaron's relief at not being in trouble with the head of the association was tempered by his curiosity.

"We've got one of the sponsors visiting this event."

Still not sure what this had to do with him, Aaron nodded. "Okay."

"I need you to play host to them for me."

Aaron lifted his brows. "Play host, like how? Which sponsor?"

"Cole Shock Absorbers."

Aaron widened his eyes at Tom's answer. "Cole?"

Cole wasn't just any corporate sponsor. They were huge. Like the biggest one of the top three that made the pro bull riding tour possible.

The company logo was on the safety vest of every rider on the circuit. The patch was right there, front and center over Aaron's heart every time he lowered himself onto the back of a bull to ride.

"Yup." Tom nodded. "I need you to hang out with the new owner during the event. Give 'em the real VIP treatment."

"Wouldn't one of the other guys be better at this?"

Aaron was thinking that Mustang Jackson would be more suited to this duty. Not only did Mustang have a golden tongue when it came to speaking to people, he was also currently ranked in the top five riders this season.

In that position, Mustang was a possible contender for the

world champion title while, after a bit of a slump the last few events, Aaron counted himself lucky that he was still hanging on to a spot in the top twenty-five.

Even Garret was ranked better than Aaron in the standings this season. Why didn't they ask him to do this? Aaron opened his mouth to suggest Garret instead, having no qualms about throwing his brother-in-law's name into the hat for this questionable assignment but didn't get a chance.

Tom shook his head and cut off Aaron's protest before he even had a chance to make it. "I want you for this. Is that a problem?"

"Uh, no. No problem at all." What the hell could Aaron say to the most powerful man in the organization? The guy who signed the big cardboard checks they all hoped to win and get photographed with at the close of every event.

"Good." Tom looked as if he was going to leave.

Aaron panicked and took a step forward. "Wait."

The man paused, brows lifted high. "Problem?"

About a dozen, but Aaron narrowed it down to the most pressing. "How am I going to recognize these Cole folks?"

The older man let out a snort. "Don't worry. I'll be around to introduce you, but you won't be able to miss them, I'm sure."

"Okay." Wondering what the hell that strange comment meant, Aaron had no choice but to remain in the dark as Tom's cell phone rang.

"I'll see you later." After a parting glance at Aaron, Tom pulled the phone out of his jacket pocket and pressed it to his ear.

As Tom walked away, Aaron was left with more questions than he'd had before. What the hell was he going to do to be a good host to these VIPs? And if he did a bad job, how much trouble would he be in?

"Aaron!"

Another summons came from behind him. He recognized the voice. This time it was Garret calling him. Aaron pivoted back to face the direction he'd been headed before the strange conversation with the boss had waylaid him.

Garret stood on the opposite side of the arena. "Come on, bro. We're going to eat."

"I'm coming."

When Aaron reached him, Garret tipped his head in the direction Tom had gone. "What was that about out there?"

Garret had obviously seen the odd meet-up out on the dirt. "Hell if I know why, but they want me to play host to the people from Cole Shock Absorbers during the event today. I guess I'm supposed to sit with them above the chutes in the VIP section when I'm between rides."

"Like glorified babysitting duty?" His brother-in-law frowned.

Aaron shrugged. "I don't know. I mean, they're a huge sponsor and have been for years. They must have been to tons of events before. Why do they need anybody at all to play tour guide now? And why *me*?"

"Pfft. Exactly," Garret agreed a little too readily and enthusiastically.

It sounded too much like an insult for Aaron's liking. Like he wasn't good enough to be their host. "Hey. I'm perfectly capable of doing it, I just don't want to."

Garret snorted. "I don't blame you. I wouldn't want to either because if you do fuck it up, I can't imagine the boss man will be very happy with you. Hell, you better not mess up or Cole could pull their sponsorship. This whole series would probably have to fold without their money."

"Jesus, Garret. Shut the hell up." As if Aaron wasn't nervous enough about this assignment, he really didn't need Garret putting shit like that into his head.

Garret stopped walking to turn to Aaron. "Just saying."

"Well, stop. Come on. I see Skeeter and Riley already waiting on us." Happy for the diversion, Aaron headed toward the bullpens at a pace fast enough Garret would have to work to keep up.

Maybe that would prevent him from talking any more.

"Ready to eat?" Skeeter asked, holding Riley's hand, just as he usually did ever since they'd started up together.

Aaron tried not to think that it could have been him standing there with Riley instead of Skeeter. But Aaron was a good friend, and being a good friend, he'd bowed out when Skeeter had told him he had a thing for Riley.

Still, had Aaron stayed in the running to win Riley, he had no doubt that today he'd be the one helping her haul the bulls to the events and running her stock contracting business.

It would be him living at Riley's ranch and sharing her bed every night, not Skeeter.

He pushed that pointless thought out of his head. Hopefully, his host duties wouldn't extend past the end of the event tonight so he could go out and have some fun.

Speaking of his host duties, he still wasn't sure when the Cole people would be arriving. Tom might expect Aaron to be there early to entertain them. "I'm ready. Let's go quick. I want to get back as soon as I can."

"Why?" Skeeter frowned at Aaron. "We have hours before the opening."

"Aaron has to babysit the Cole Shock Absorbers people."

Skeeter's eyes widened at Garret's announcement. "Wow."

Riley's brow creased beneath the brim of her cowboy hat. "Hmm, I just read something online about that company the other day."

"Really? What?" Aaron wanted to go in to this duty armed with any information he could get his hands on.

"The owners got a divorce. Somehow the wife walked away owning Cole Shocks and the husband wasn't at all happy. I don't know all the details, but they went to court over it and he lost."

"So you mean Aaron has to play tour guide to Mrs. Cole, not Mr.?" Garret laughed. "Oh, man. Now I think I'm kind of envious you got that assignment instead of me."

Aaron frowned. "Why?"

Garret let out a short laugh. "Don't you know?"

"No. That's why I asked." Jesus, sometimes his brother-in-law could really try Aaron's patience.

"CeCe Cole is hot. She was a famous super model. That was like twenty years ago, but she still looks pretty damn good to me."

Aaron scowled. "I'm sure your wife, my sister, would be real thrilled to hear that you think so."

Garret dismissed Aaron with the wave of one hand. "You can't scare me. Nowadays, Silver doesn't care what I think as long as I keep getting up in the middle of the night to give the baby a bottle so she can sleep."

Boy, times had changed. Just a year ago, any middle-of-the-night activities involving bottles and babes were of a completely different kind from what Garret was talking about now.

Aaron loved his new nephew Jackson with all his heart, but he still thanked God that the birth of his sister's baby hadn't changed his life. At least not as dramatically as it had changed things for Garret and Silver.

He was looking forward to a few bottles of beer and a hot babe tonight. In fact, he'd get right on that after the event, as soon as he was done babysitting CeCe Cole.

CHAPTER TWO

Inside the cool, dim interior, Jill Malone waited for the driver to open the limo's rear door.

The photographer she'd hired was already outside waiting for them. Currently, he was backing away from the car, camera raised and ready as he lined up the angle. He knew to make sure he didn't miss any good shots as CeCe slid out of the backseat and stepped into the brilliant late afternoon sunlight.

As the former wife of corporate mogul John Cole, CeCe Cole never arrived anywhere without making a splashy entrance—not even to a bull ride.

As Jill moved to get out of the car after her boss, CeCe glanced back and extended one hand, palm up. "Sunglasses."

Jill glanced around her in the limo. Sure enough, the large-framed designer sunglasses were in a cup holder, right where CeCe must have stuck them. She grabbed them and put them in CeCe's hand.

The tall, willowy redhead made even putting on sunglasses look practiced. She slid them on slowly with one hand while the other hand rested on the hip stuck out to one side.

Once a model, always a model, Jill supposed. Even if it

had been close to twenty-five years since CeCe had graced a runway. She hadn't needed to. Not once she'd married John Cole and his millions.

Still standing next to the car, CeCe looked around through the dark lenses of the glasses. Jill could only imagine she was appalled at the sight surrounding them.

This wasn't exactly the red carpet at the Academy Awards. There were no paparazzi. No stars. No crowds of bull-riding fans even.

Hours before the start of the professional bull-riding event, there wasn't much more to see outside the arena entrance than a few trucks in the parking lot. There wasn't much chance of being seen either, so CeCe's showy entrance was for nothing.

"This is it?" CeCe asked. She glanced back to where Jill waited, poised on the edge of the bench seat since CeCe had yet to move out of the doorway.

Jill resisted the urge to laugh at the question. "This is it."

CeCe Cole was definitely out of her comfort zone here. Luckily for all of them, Jill was smack in the middle of hers. Her father had been a competitive roper, and her grandfather before him. She'd been going to rodeos for as long as she could remember.

"Where are all the spectators? I thought bull riding was a popular sport."

"It is. It's still early. The crowd will be here soon. I promise."

"Well, I certainly hope we're going to be indoors with air conditioning. It's hot as blazes out here." Finally, CeCe stepped away from the limo and toward the building's doors.

Jill stopped herself from commenting that of course it was hot. They were in Georgia. Instead she took the opportunity to finally slip out of the car. Reaching back in, she grabbed her oversized bag from the seat. She slipped the strap over her shoulder and then had to scramble to catch up with CeCe. Her boss had crazy long legs and could move fast when she chose to.

"So what's on the agenda?" CeCe spoke as she climbed the staircase to the entrance doors.

"First, we'll take some pictures."

"Fine. Where do you want me?"

Jill knew the prospect of being the center of attention would make CeCe happy. She never had been able to resist a camera lens. "In front of the chute with the Cole banner."

Inside the building, CeCe halted and turned to Jill. "All I see are beer vendors and greasy fast food stands. How do we get to this chute? And why has no one from the organization come to greet us yet?"

"I'm sure they will soon. This is the concourse. We have to go down to the arena floor for the chutes. Come on. I'll show you where." Explaining was pointless since she could see CeCe had already stopped listening.

Jill motioned to the photographer, knowing where the camera went CeCe would surely follow. She dug their VIP full-access passes out of her bag and flashed them at the security guard before leading the way down a few flights of steep stairs.

She drew in the pre-event smells of the arena—mainly bulls and shit. Glancing back, she saw CeCe wrinkle her nose. Jill turned away to hide her smile.

Manure was definitely not an odor CeCe was familiar with. Nature and the great outdoors wasn't her thing. The closest CeCe had ever gotten to the horse crowd was at a catered fundraiser to benefit some equine organization.

Teetering in expensive designer heels much too high and completely impractical given the venue, CeCe picked her way across the arena dirt to stand in front of the chute bearing her corporate name and logo.

"Uck. There is absolutely nothing I hate more than dirt. Isn't there anywhere else to take pictures? Like from up there?" CeCe waved a hand at the platform above them.

"You're already down here. You might as well take the pictures and be done with it."

CeCe rolled her eyes and let out a breath. "Fine. Take it."

Meanwhile, Jill was probably going to be the one who cleaned CeCe's shoes anyway.

The photographer jogged back a few feet and then turned to raise the camera. CeCe smiled for the shot and, like magic, it was as if an entirely different person stood before them.

A few clicks later and the photographer lowered the camera again. "That should do it."

"Thank God." The smile was quickly replaced by a scowl as she glanced at Jill. "Why are we taking these pictures again?"

As the manager of media and public relations for Cole Shock Absorbers, Jill could have gone into the many reasons why it was important to show the public that, even though John Cole no longer owned the company, CeCe was going to be just as active as he had been.

How as a company they needed CeCe to be tied to the corporate branding as strongly as John had been.

How it never hurt to have an attractive woman associated with a product when the main consumers of that product were male.

Jill knew most of her reasoning would be lost on CeCe, so she decided to break it down to the bare bones.

"These are to post on our social media sites." When CeCe raised one perfectly shaped and dyed red eyebrow, Jill added, "And to rub it in Mr. Cole's face that you now own controlling interest in his favorite company, which also sponsors one of his favorite sports."

CeCe's smile appeared again, shining bright and taking years off her age. If CeCe would only smile more often, she could pass for far younger than her fifty-one years. Although no one dared even breathe that number.

There was an unspoken rule among those in the inner circle that CeCe Cole would never age past forty-something. At least not as far as any Cole Shocks employees were concerned—not if they wanted to remain employed.

The media was another story altogether. Jill spent a considerable amount of her time making sure CeCe didn't get her hands on any articles that touted her real age.

In CeCe's defense, she had aged well. She was still as firm and slender as she'd always been.

Staying in shape was a priority for her, but she didn't go overboard and keep herself too thin, knowing that would have made her look older. She never went in the sun without sunscreen or a hat. And though Jill suspected CeCe might have gotten some help from plastic surgeons, it was subtle. Not at all obvious like some aging women in the public eye who tried to look younger.

There was no doubt CeCe Cole was an attractive woman and she knew it and expected to be treated accordingly. Luckily, most men were eager to comply.

Speaking of men—Jill was more than a little relieved to see Tom Parsons, the head of the bull-riding organization, heading toward them. If CeCe's presence had been ignored any longer, there might have been hell to pay and, deserved or not, Jill would have been the one to take the heat.

"CeCe." Jill touched her boss's arm to get her attention. "Tom Parsons from the association is here."

"It's about time." The snark in CeCe's attitude disappeared as soon as Tom was within hearing distance. She donned her trademark smile that only those closest to her recognized as being completely fake. "Hello. So nice to finally meet you, Mr. Parsons."

"Please, call me Tom."

CeCe extended her hand to the man. "And you must call me CeCe."

"Yes, ma'am." He took CeCe's offered hand and shook it. "I'm so happy you could come to our event."

"My pleasure, though I usually do like my sporting events a little less . . . dirty." CeCe glanced pointedly down at the arena dirt, into which her high spiked heels had long ago sunken deep.

He laughed, looking completely charmed by CeCe. "Be glad it's before the competition. Afterward, there's more than just dirt on the arena floor."

"Yes, of course." CeCe's laugh tinkled charmingly, though Jill was pretty sure Tom's alluding to the bull snot and shit that would soon be intermingled with the dirt was lost on her.

CeCe Cole didn't tend to think about inconvenient things that were usually taken care of by hired help, such as disposing of manure. The bullshit CeCe usually dealt in was of a different variety.

Clearly under CeCe's spell, Tom finally released his hold on CeCe's hand.

Since it didn't look as if her boss was going to bother introducing her, Jill took a step forward. "Mr. Parsons, I'm Jill Malone. We've been emailing back and forth for the past few weeks regarding this visit."

"Of course. Pleasure to meet you, Ms. Malone."

Jill noticed as she shook his hand that the man didn't suggest she call him Tom the way he had with CeCe. Nor did he take quite as long to release his hold on her as he had with her former-model boss.

What else was new? Jill was used to this. Women like CeCe, with flaming-red hair, an over-the-top personality and the body to go with it, always got treated differently than girls who blended in with the crowd like Jill did.

She didn't mind. It was just one reason why CeCe had made a successful living in front of the camera, while Jill was much more comfortable and productive being behind the scenes.

"Shall we go on up?" Tom asked, gesturing to the stands. "We can get you something to drink or eat before the event starts if you'd like."

"That would be lovely." Before CeCe was able to hide it, Jill saw the look of shock and horror on CeCe's face at the thought of eating or drinking anything from the fast food vendors they'd passed on the concourse.

The woman was always concerned with maintaining her figure, and picky about everything, food included. Keeping CeCe happy and finding something for her to eat on the road was always a challenge, even when they were at the finest restaurants.

As they walked, Tom continued talking, unaware that the nearer they got to the beer and nacho window, the more horrified CeCe would become. "I've arranged for one of the bull riders to stay with you during the event to explain the sport."

"Oh, really?" The genuine interest resonating through CeCe's comment had Jill pausing. Being given a bull rider all of her own was the first thing CeCe had looked enthusiastic about since arriving.

Apparently, good old Tom was no dummy when it came to manipulating women. In particular, recently divorced women newly in control of their ex-husband's large corporation and its sponsorship funds.

"Aaron Jordan. He's here somewhere." Tom looked around them. "In fact, let me text my assistant and see if he's in the rider room. I'll have him come up and join us."

As Tom pulled his cell out of his suit pocket to no doubt summon the bull rider, CeCe smiled. "That sounds lovely. Thank you."

This time, CeCe's smile looked completely genuine at the mention of the cowboy whose job for the night was to tend solely to her. CeCe loved nothing more than being the center of attention. If that attention originated from a handsome male, even better.

Jill was pretty pleased with the situation herself. She could have explained the sport to CeCe, but it was doubtful her boss would have been interested enough to care to hear about it. But with one of the bull riders doing the explaining, CeCe was sure to be all ears. Jill's evening just got a whole lot easier.

CHAPTER THREE

Aaron leaned back from the table, resisting the temptation to polish off the rest of the fries. He really shouldn't stuff himself right before a ride. If he finished what was on his plate, he'd be full enough to bust a gut.

Really good french fries were his weakness. A temptation he couldn't resist.

Hell, why was he resisting anyway? There was still a bit of time left before he had to ride and the fries were too damn good to let go to waste. He'd just reached for one more fry when an incoming call made his cell phone light up and vibrate on the table.

Aaron didn't recognize the number on the readout, but he hit to answer it anyway and pressed the phone to his ear. It could be a girl he'd given his number to at a past event. He had no intention of missing that.

"Hello?"

"Jordan, where are you?"

Aaron drew his brows low at the sound of a man's voice. "Who is this?"

"It's Tom Parsons."

Tom Parsons? What the hell? First the boss was asking

Aaron for favors, and now the man had his cell phone number and was calling him? What sort of weird shit was going on today?

Garret, Chase, Skeeter and Riley all watched Aaron as he said, "Oh, hey. I'm just finishing up eating."

"I need you back at the arena, ASAP."

"Um, okay. We just gotta get the bill and pay—"

"Just get here right away. The Cole folks have arrived."

Shit. He hadn't even started his assignment yet and he was already fucking it up.

"All right. I'll be there as soon as I can." Aaron disconnected the call and glanced up at his friends. "I gotta get back right away."

"Why? We've got plenty of time." Chase looked down at the time displayed on the face of his cell phone.

Aaron scowled. "It looks like my babysitting—or former model-sitting—is starting early."

"Your what?" Chase frowned.

"Aaron has to play hostess for the Cole Shock Absorbers people. I'll find the waitress and get the bill." Skeeter squeezed Riley's hand on the table before he stood. "I'll be right back."

She smiled sweetly. "Okay."

Aaron resisted the urge to roll his eyes that these two couldn't even be apart for thirty seconds without a big goodbye scene.

Next to Aaron, Garret turned in his chair. "I sure hope you get something outta this gig Tom Parsons gave you."

"Like what?" Aaron asked.

"Like the name Cole Shock Absorbers embroidered down the arm of your riding shirt and a big old sponsor check in your bank account, that's what."

More sponsor money to help cover expenses would be nice. With the cost of travel seeming to go up every time he booked a flight or filled his truck with fuel, Aaron sure as hell wouldn't say no to a Cole check.

Aaron looked for Skeeter with the bill. He had to get

moving. He was getting anxious that he was falling down on the duties assigned him by the boss.

"Dude. You're hopping around in your chair like you've got ants in your pants. Go. I'll take care of the bill and Chase can give me, Skeeter and Riley a ride back."

"You sure?" Aaron turned to Chase to confirm. "That all right with you?"

Chase nodded. "Of course. I got room in my truck."

"All right. Thanks. I'll feel better once I get over there." It wasn't every day a rider got an assignment, or a phone call, from Tom Parsons personally. Pushing his chair back, Aaron stood. "See y'all there."

"Yup. Then you'll have to introduce us to the lovely former Mrs. Cole." Aaron ignored Garret's comment and strode toward the door, but it had him wondering, what was he supposed to call her?

If it had been an ugly divorce, like Riley said, was calling her *Mrs. Cole* even appropriate? Aaron didn't know her maiden name. What he did know was that he was completely out of his comfort zone in the role of ambassador of the association, but there wasn't much he could do about it.

Concerned with the time, he jogged for the truck in the parking lot. He probably risked getting a ticket by speeding to the arena, but he got there safe and sound and without any flashing police lights behind him, so it was all good.

The front lot was getting busy. Even this long before show time, fans would start cruising the lot, looking for the perfect parking place for their cars and trucks.

People were already streaming between the rows of parked vehicles. A lot of them were families with kids in tow. It was nice that bull riding was a family sport, but Aaron didn't have time to navigate at a crawl through the chaos and worry about a kid running out in front of his truck. He had to park and find Tom Parsons—and Mrs. Cole Shock Absorbers.

He pulled directly around to the side of the building to where the riders had their vehicles. He threw the truck into park and hopped out, pocketing his keys. Striding past trucks and trailers, he headed for the rear door.

While walking past the bull pens, Aaron kept his eye out for anyone who looked like they might be a former super model and new owner of the largest corporate sponsor on the tour.

He didn't see anyone except stock handlers.

"Hey, Clint. You guys see Tom Parsons bringing a woman around back here?"

"Nope." Clint lifted a brow. "Why? Is Parsons into impressing the buckle bunnies with behind-the-scenes tours now?"

Jesus, Clint spreading rumors about the head of the association because of Aaron's one innocent but poorly worded question was the last thing anyone needed.

Aaron scrambled to clear things up. "No. She's a sponsor. I thought maybe he was showing her the bulls or something."

Though now that Clint had mentioned it, a behind-the-scenes tour wasn't a bad idea. If Aaron ran out of things to talk to her about, he might consider it.

Would a rich divorcee like that? What the hell did Aaron know? He hung around with guys and girls from his own world. He didn't generally rub elbows with multi-millionaires.

Drawing in a breath as his task seemed more daunting than ever, Aaron headed for the arena. If he didn't find the Cole people soon, he'd have to call Tom back and ask where they were.

They could be in some green room where the association mucky-mucks hung out. He didn't know what those people did while he was behind the chutes with the other riders. He'd never had any reason to care, until now.

"Jordan!"

This time, unlike before, hearing his name shouted across the arena was a welcome interruption. Glancing up, Aaron spotted Tom waving at him from the VIP seating above the chutes.

Show time. At least for him. The actual bull riding wouldn't start for a little while yet.

Aaron lifted one arm in a wave and strode across the dirt. He still had to get his gear bag from the rider room. Clean and rosin his rope. Strap on his spurs and his chaps, and get ready for the opening.

He wasn't nearly ready, but it didn't seem as if Tom cared about that.

The man stepped forward as Aaron reached the top of the stairs. "Aaron Jordon, this is CeCe Cole. CeCe, Aaron is one of the top riders in the world."

Aaron tipped his hat. "Nice to meet you, ma'am."

An older redhead shot him a smoldering smile with lips painted blood red. "You too."

"And this is CeCe's assistant . . ." Tom continued the introductions but stopped when it came to actually providing the younger woman's name.

"Jill." A pretty brunette took a step forward, arm extended. She shot Tom a glance. "And technically I'm manager of media and public relations."

"Nice to meet you." Aaron smiled and shook her offered hand. "And technically I'm only one of the top twenty-five riders in the world currently so . . ."

Tom didn't look all that pleased at Aaron's revelation as he continued, "I've got a couple of things to do in the back, but Aaron's going to stay with you all for the event. If there is anything you need that he can't get for you, just call. Aaron has my phone number and so does . . ."

"Jill." Jill smiled indulgently.

Tom nodded and focused again on CeCe Cole. "Either one of them can give me a call if you need me."

CeCe leveled a heated gaze at Aaron. She started at his boots and worked her way up, all the way to his hat. "I think Aaron can provide me with everything I desire."

She came across as quite the cougar, but Aaron figured she had to be joking. There was no way a woman who looked like her would be interested in a struggling bull rider half her age.

CeCe Cole was the perfect example of polished

sophistication, while Aaron was dressed in old boots and dusty jeans. She was powerful and rich and could probably buy anything she wanted. Aaron was happy just to be able to pay all his bills every month with a little left over.

Even so, it was nice of her to pretend to flirt with him.

"Yes, ma'am." Aaron laughed. He liked when women had a good sense of humor.

CeCe leaned closer. "You might think I'm kidding, but I assure you I'm not."

He opened his mouth but had no idea what to say. As both Tom and Jill watched, Aaron finally managed to respond. "Yes, ma'am."

"All right then. I'll leave you in Aaron's capable hands." Tom nodded his goodbye and left, just when Aaron wished he'd stay.

Then there was only Jill, wide-eyed and looking like she'd rather be anywhere rather than there. He didn't hold much hope that she'd save him from whatever CeCe requested of him. He was starting to suspect that might be a lot more than a tour, especially when CeCe trailed a finger down his arm.

"So, what do cowboys like you do for fun?"

"Um, not much. You know. Hang out. Ride bulls." He shrugged.

"I've got something you can ride." She smiled like the devil was inside her and continued to run one long fingernail over the sleeve of his shirt.

Wow. What to say to that?

Shocked, he was having trouble coming up with a single response. No surprise there, thanks to the distraction of her sultry low voice near his ear and the feel of those nails scraping his flesh even through the cotton of his shirt.

He was so tense the phone vibrating in his pocket had him jumping.

"Uh, excuse me a sec." He pulled out the cell and saw a text from the same number Tom had called him from.

'I want Mrs. Cole happy. Whatever she wants you give her. Understand?'

The text only ramped up Aaron's already agitated state. Swallowing hard, he shoved the cell back into his pocket before CeCe, standing much too closely, read it.

Glancing up, he noticed her watching him. "Um, that was nothing important."

Nope. Not important, unless he thought about all those few sentences implied and meant to his future career with this organization.

She smiled, her lids heavy over deep blue eyes as she flipped a long fall of thick red hair over her shoulder. "Good. I wouldn't want you to have to leave."

"Nope, I'm not leaving." Not if he wanted to keep the head of the association happy.

"Good." As she latched on to his arm with both hands and hung on, he began to wonder if she was going to let him go long enough for him to ride.

Not knowing how much rich city folk knew about bull riding, he figured he'd better bring up the subject. "I'll have to run down for the intro though."

"Okay. Then you'll come right back and stay here?"

"Yup, until I have to ride. But I'm not riding until the fifth section."

"You won't be gone too long, will you?" she asked.

"Nope. Not too long. Just eight seconds if all goes well." He forced a laugh at his own lame joke.

She lifted one perfectly shaped red brow. "I certainly hope that's the only thing that will just last eight seconds tonight."

Holy shit. Aaron could talk a pair of jeans off a female within the span of two drinks. Sometimes less. Unfortunately, it appeared he was not equally as skilled in convincing this woman to let him keep his pants on.

His heart pounded, pumping blood to other parts of him. Parts that liked the idea of what she was suggesting, whether he could wrap his brain around it or not. "Yes, ma'am."

CHAPTER FOUR

Tom Parsons had provided them great seats, as befitted a sponsor the size of Cole Shock Absorbers.

From the VIP seating right above the chutes, Jill could see all the action happening out on the dirt, and also what was going on before and after the rides behind the chutes.

In this area, they could choose to sit or stand along the rail to get an even better view.

Before the event started, Jill had been able to look down and see all the riders getting prepared for the event—including Aaron Jordan. That had been the one time CeCe had let go of his arm. Even then it had only been long enough for him to run down and take care of business.

Now that the event was in full swing, Aaron was back at his post next to CeCe along the rail while his fellow competitors were down below them.

Determined to not stare at CeCe's embarrassing show of affection toward the cowboy half her age who she'd only met that night, Jill tried to watch what was happening below instead.

A few guys were stretching, likely because they were about to ride in the next section, which would be the fourth of the night. One young cowboy slipped a safety helmet on and strapped it beneath his chin right before climbing into the chute.

Some guys wore helmets to ride and some didn't. Jill could see another rider clamp his cowboy hat tighter onto his head while he balanced on the rails above the back of the bull within the narrow metal chute.

Aaron was watching this section intently. He faced the action, gripping the rail with both hands. He was pretty much ignoring CeCe as she sidled up next to him, holding on to his forearm as strongly as Aaron held the rail in front of him.

The rider in the helmet called out, "Go!"

A gateman pulled a rope that swung the chute open before he scrambled to the side.

The big, horned bull leapt into the arena, surprisingly agile and quick on his feet considering his size. The animal settled into a spin as the rider balanced atop him.

Aaron leaned forward as he watched, shouting encouragement to rider. "Go, go, go!"

The sound of the eight-second buzzer cut through the air and the crowd reacted. A collective cheer reverberated off the walls as the bull continued to spin.

The rider reached down and pulled the tail of the bull rope wrapped around his riding hand. The rope released and he leapt to the ground on the outside of the spin. The three bull fighters in the arena moved in to draw the animal's attention while the rider ran for the rails and leapt onto the metal gate of an empty chute.

Jill held her breath until the rider was safe, but she needn't have worried. The bull had stopped its motion shortly after the rider jumped off. Now, it stood in the center, pivoting to look for the exit. When the out gate swung wide, the bull trotted through.

The rider finally pulled off his helmet, grinning wide that he'd covered the ride.

"Aaron, I asked you a question." The displeasure in CeCe's tone was clear to Jill.

Apparently, CeCe's annoyance was clear to Aaron, as well. He turned immediately away from the rail to face CeCe. "I'm sorry. I just wanted to see that one ride. That was my friend Skeeter."

"Oh. Well, he did fine, didn't he?"

Aaron wobbled his head back and forth. "Eh, we'll see when the score comes up."

Jill shook her head. "Yeah. He made the whistle, but I'm not sure the score will be high enough for him to place. The bull was a real flat bucker. He probably should have tried to dress up the ride a little bit so he'd score better."

At her unsolicited evaluation of his friend's ride, Aaron's gaze whipped to Jill.

She cringed that he might be offended. She'd basically just criticized his friend's riding. "Sorry. It was a good ride though."

"Eighty-two-point-five for Skeeter Anderson. Not enough to put him on the leader board for tonight's event." The announcer's amplified voice bounced off the walls just as the numbers flashed on the big screen high above the arena.

Aaron shook his head. "Don't apologize. You were dead on. He had a cold streak a few months back so he needs all the points he can get before the Finals. Tonight won't add as much as he'd like. Not if he can't ride in the short go."

"Yeah, I remember when he was riding in the Touring Pro Division for a while. Those extra points from the final round would have been nice to have."

Aaron looked at Jill with even more interest than before. As if he was really noticing her for the first time. "You follow the sport?"

"Of course." Out of the corner of her eye, Jill saw the unhappy expression on her boss's face.

The one thing that irked CeCe the most was not being the center of attention. Jill had made the unforgivable faux pas of drawing some of Aaron's attention away from CeCe.

Instead of telling him she'd been going to rodeos since before she could walk or that she'd been mutton bustin' at five years old, she scrambled to make it right.

With as casual a shrug as she could manage, Jill said, "But I'm very happy you're here to explain the finer points to CeCe since I'd never be able to do it as well. Um, for instance, maybe you could tell CeCe what that rider is doing over there?"

Aaron swiveled to glance in the direction Jill had indicated, where a Brazilian rider was bouncing up and down, going from a squat to standing repeatedly.

Jill knew damn well he was warming up his muscles for his ride, but Aaron explaining it to CeCe would go a long way to soothe her ruffled feathers.

"Oh, sure. He's just warming up and stretching. We riders don't always break bones when we're out on the injured list. Sometimes it's just from stuff like a pulled groin muscle."

"Oh, my. We definitely don't want *that* to happen tonight. Make sure you stretch very well before you ride." CeCe grabbed right on to the topic of Aaron's groin, twisting it into a flirtation.

It was just as Jill expected from her, and it worked perfectly for Jill to extricate herself from the spotlight and thrust her boss back into it.

Truth be told, she had enjoyed basking in the warm glow of Aaron's attention for the short time she'd gotten to experience it. Sad that the plain girl next door that she was couldn't outshine a woman twice her age. Sure, CeCe was a rich, powerful, beautiful woman, but still it kind of hurt.

Even if Jill could out-flirt CeCe, to do so would mean a guaranteed spot on the unemployment line.

Glancing at Aaron, with his brilliant eyes so deep blue they seemed almost violet beneath his dark auburn brows, Jill had to wonder if losing her job over him might be worth it.

The strength of his jawline drew her attention as Jill watched him turn to CeCe to answer some question she'd asked. The fantasy of running her lips over that chin on the way to his mouth hit her hard.

CeCe leaned closer to him, hooking her fingers through

his belt loops. He didn't move away. In fact, he rested one hand on CeCe's shoulder and leaned in to point something in the arena out to her.

Yup, even if it had appeared that he'd started the night surprised at CeCe's hardcore pursuit of him, it seemed he'd settled into it quite nicely now.

Jill sighed and decided she might as well check her email for lack of anything else to do while they waited for the next section to start.

The freelance photographer they'd hired to do the publicity shots when they'd first arrived had already uploaded the photos and sent her the link.

At least she'd have something to do tonight after the event. She sure as hell wouldn't have CeCe to entertain. Aaron was clearly going to take care of that.

Jill should probably be grateful for Aaron relieving her of CeCe duty for the night. She wasn't. Not even close.

"I'm afraid I'm going to have to leave you for a little bit. I gotta go downstairs and get ready for my ride."

Jill felt an overwhelming sense of relief at Aaron's announcement he was leaving for a bit, even if it was said for CeCe's benefit and not her own. If CeCe got any closer to Aaron, she'd end up inside his clothes with him.

"All right. But come right back when you're done?"

"Yes, ma'am."

CeCe finally released him from her clutches.

Thank goodness. The woman was bordering on being inappropriately handsy with him in what was a very public venue. There were other people in the VIP area with them and the television cameras were rolling.

Aaron turned to leave. He'd only taken one step toward the stairs before CeCe called after him, "I'll be cheering for you."

"Thanks." Aaron didn't stop, but continued down the stairs as he spoke.

Jill felt a little too satisfied at how unhappy CeCe looked that he'd left her side.

Maybe Jill was a little envious of her boss. Hell, what woman wouldn't be? Aaron was a good-looking man, not to mention a good bull rider with a bright future . . . in a sport CeCe cared nothing about.

Jill fought the scowl that last thought brought on and stepped closer to her boss, ready to take over entertaining her again. It wasn't in her job description, but it had become clear to Jill rather quickly that handling CeCe would be as big a part of her position as handling social media and the press.

"The riders can get disqualified if they're not ready when their turn comes." When CeCe looked at her with a blank expression, Jill continued, "That's why Aaron had to leave early for his ride. To make sure he was ready in time."

She lifted one red brow. "Believe me, I'm quite sure he wouldn't have left my side if he didn't absolutely have to."

All righty.

After that remark, that was the last thing Jill intended to explain to CeCe for the duration of the event.

CHAPTER FIVE

"So . . ." When Garret let that single word dangle with no follow up, Aaron was forced to take his attention off the chaps in his hand, the ones he needed to put on before his ride.

Aaron glanced up from the chap strap buckles. "Is there a question in there somewhere?"

"Yes. How are things going with Ms. Cole Shocks?" That question from Garret was definitely not as casual as it seemed.

If Aaron hadn't figured that out immediately from Garret's tone alone, he would have from his pointed stare in the direction of the VIP seating.

"Things are going fine." Aaron glanced up at the seats above the chutes.

He didn't spot CeCe along the rail. Only Jill. That was a relief. At least Garret wouldn't be able to ogle CeCe and get them all in trouble with Tom. Aaron didn't need anything else to worry about. He had to get ready for his ride and do it fast too.

Turning his concentration back to his pre-ride prep, Aaron worked extra hard to ignore Garret, hoping to squelch any further questions about a subject he didn't want to talk about.

It was apparent that Tom Parsons expected Aaron to keep CeCe Cole happy. Just as it was becoming more and more obvious that his efforts to keep CeCe happy would not end after the final bull ride of the event.

He wasn't sure how to feel about getting pimped out. CeCe was hot for her age. If the situation were different, if he'd seen her in the stands, he definitely would have taken a second look.

So why did this feel wrong? Aaron knew the answer to that. Because it hadn't been his idea. Because it felt like it was expected of him. And what CeCe expected was more than he ever thought he'd be asked by his association to give.

Maybe he was reading the situation all wrong. Of course Tom wouldn't require him or even expect him to go home with CeCe tonight. That would be crazy.

Tom probably meant that Aaron should make sure CeCe was happy during the event. Like if she got hungry or thirsty, Aaron should get her something.

And if she was hungry for Aaron himself? Then what?

An image of CeCe stripping off her already-revealing clothes hit him just as he was trying to get his head on straight before his ride.

He shoved the thought aside to make room for what was most important—his ride.

If he climbed into that chute with his little head doing the thinking, Aaron could very well end up being taken out of the arena on a stretcher. Then nobody would be happy. Not CeCe Cole. Not Tom Parsons. Certainly not Aaron himself.

He pushed aside all thoughts of CeCe Cole, naked or otherwise.

Garret, arms folded as he watched Aaron, said, "So we're all going out after the event. There's a bar right next to the hotel."

"Who all is going?" Aaron asked.

"The usual crew. Skeeter and Riley. Me. Chase."

Aaron frowned. "Riley's not twenty-one yet. She's not

legal to get into a bar."

"Skeeter found out the place has a full menu so they let everyone in. She just can't order a drink." Garret lifted his shoulder in a shrug. "She doesn't like to drink anyway. And since when are you the liquor police?"

"I'm not. I was just wondering." Aaron tried to seem casual as he deflected the conversation away from him and on to Riley so Garret wouldn't notice Aaron never said he'd be there.

He couldn't promise to go out with the guys in case he was needed elsewhere. Somewhere with CeCe. She wouldn't go for the bar across from the hotel where he was sharing a seventy-nine-dollar-a-night room with Garret and Chase. She'd want him to take her somewhere better . . . or to her hotel room.

And why was he thinking that? Maybe she was just being friendly. Or yeah, she was flirting, but maybe she never meant for him to think it would go anywhere. She was so much older than he was and she was newly divorced.

Aaron glanced up again and saw Jill still alone as she looked over the rail. She worked for CeCe. Maybe Jill would have some insight into her boss. Like about how CeCe usually acted with men. In particular, men whose asses she liked to rest her hand on when she talked to them.

He couldn't ask Jill outright, but maybe he could hint around a little. But how embarrassing would that be if he was totally off the mark and CeCe was only being friendly?

Aaron didn't need to look like an idiot in front of Jill. She was cute—the kind of girl he'd totally go for if he wasn't being overwhelmed by all the attention from CeCe Cole.

"Why do you look so miserable?" Garret's question brought Aaron out of his thoughts and back to the present.

"I'm not."

"Yeah, you are. Come on. Spill. Talk to me." Garret leveled a stare at Aaron. He even sounded sincerely concerned for once.

Aaron glanced up at the VIP section and back again. "It's

CeCe Cole."

"What about her?"

"I don't know what to make of her."

A wrinkle creased Garret's brow. "I don't know what you mean."

"She's real flirty. Like some of the things she says . . ." Aaron shook his head. "I don't know if she means them the way they sound or not, but it could be taken as kinda *dirty*. And she's always touching me."

Garret's eyes widened. "Can you hear yourself talking?"

"Yeah. Why?"

"If I came to you and said a hot, rich, former model was flirting, talking dirty and had her hands all over me, what the hell would you tell me to do?"

"But this isn't a normal woman. She's the tour's biggest sponsor."

"Sponsors have needs too." Garret grinned.

Aaron scowled. "Thanks a lot. You're a real big help."

"Seriously, bro. Just go with it. Let her lead and you follow."

That was actually good advice. If he let her take the lead, then he couldn't fuck it up. If she asked him to do something after the event, he'd say yes. If she didn't, he'd say goodbye and that would be it.

"Okay. That's a good plan. Thanks." Aaron's head was still spinning with possible scenarios when he noticed Garret watching him. "What?"

"You gonna finish buckling your chap straps or are you planning to ride with them flapping around loose like that?"

Mumbling a cuss, Aaron reached for the leather strap he'd forgotten to buckle.

Garret let out a snort. "Damn. Ms. Shock Absorber has really gotten to you."

"I'll be fine for the ride." Aaron could have handled CeCe Cole and her flirting a hell of a lot better if he wasn't afraid of messing things up and pissing off Tom Parsons.

"You'd better be. You're on Bad to the Bone. You know

he's rank, bro."

"I know. You don't have to remind me." Aaron was well aware of the bull's reputation and eighty-five percent buck-off rate. But the riders who did make eight scored high. That's what Aaron was hoping for.

"I just don't want you landing face down in the dirt and looking bad in front of your admirer."

Aaron blew out a breath. "I can't really worry about that, now can I? You know damn well face-planting in the dirt could happen whether I cover the ride or not. But CeCe doesn't seem to follow bull riding, so she probably doesn't know that."

"I wasn't talking about Ms. Cole."

"What are you talking about?" Aaron asked.

"The pretty young thing who hasn't taken her eyes off you since you came down."

"What pretty young thing?" Frowning, Aaron turned to see who Garret was talking about.

"The cute brunette dressed way too fancy for a bull ride and hanging over the rail of the VIP section to get a look at you putting on your chaps."

"Jill?" Aaron dismissed Garret. "She's the Cole Shocks marketing person. That's all."

"No, man. I don't think that's all. She's interested."

"You're nuts." Aaron glanced up again and sure enough, Jill was looking his way. "She's probably just supposed to watch for her job."

"Yeah, whatever."

"Whatever." Aaron sighed, not knowing what to think anymore.

It didn't matter if Jill was watching him. This CeCe situation had him all confused, not to mention frustrated.

Usually, he loved women. Loved everything about them. How they smelled, so fresh and clean. How they felt, so smooth and soft beneath his hands. Everything.

Usually . . . but not today. If someone had told him yesterday that he'd be this thrown just from some female attention, he'd never have believed them, but that was exactly how he felt.

He grabbed his vest from the rail. "Come on."

"Where we going?"

"Over to my chute." Aaron needed to get clear of the estrogen in this arena for a bit and be surrounded by men for a little while. He needed a big dose of male companionship before he got on the bull, and before he had to go back up and be surrounded by the most confusing creatures ever created—women.

CHAPTER SIX

The flash of fringe below was what had caught Jill's attention in the first place as Aaron slung a pair of chaps around his hips. He'd buckled them at the waist and then secured them around each one of his thighs.

It shouldn't have been hot, but it was. The denim. The leather. The hat. The boots. The shadow of stubble on the strong chin. It was a deadly combination. One Jill shouldn't be noticing.

There was no way CeCe was letting Aaron out of her clutches, even if he had been at all interested in Jill. But it was sure nice to watch and fantasize. Aaron Jordan would definitely give Jill something to think about when she was lying alone in bed tonight.

"I'm going to the ladies' room." CeCe's announcement broke into Jill's fantasy.

She glanced down again. Aaron had already donned his safety vest and was currently climbing the rails of one of the chutes loaded with a bull. "But Aaron's about to ride."

"I won't be long." CeCe dismissed Jill's concern with the flick of one wrist.

A better person might have told CeCe that if she left now,

she was going to miss Aaron's ride no matter how quick she was. A good employee might even have offered to go with her boss.

Jill wasn't that person. Instead she said, "All right."

She let CeCe go and then turned back to watch the action. She was just in time to see the bull in Aaron's chute hop up and almost get its front legs over the rail. She gasped as Aaron hovered, straddling the rails above the unruly animal.

Aaron climbed back to one side as another rider appeared with a rope. He looped it so it spanned the front and back rails, forming a barrier, however flimsy, above the bull's neck. The animal hopped again, but the cowboy held the rope firm.

Amazingly, the rope worked. The bull bumped the rope above him and that little bit of resistance made him settle back onto all four feet.

Aaron moved to climb onto the animal's back again. Jill held her breath, willing the bull to behave.

The chute was a dangerous place. Deep and narrow. Small and confined. Basically not much more than a topless metal cage containing well over a thousand pounds of bucking bull and one human a tenth of its size.

As the man in the chute next to Aaron's took off into the arena for his own ride, Aaron began to wrap his rope around his gloved hand. A few seconds later, the other rider was in the dirt before the buzzer sounded.

Things moved fast in this sport. As soon as the bucked-off rider and his bull were clear of the arena, it would be Aaron's turn to ride. And unless CeCe was back from the bathroom, she was going to miss it.

That was CeCe's own fault. Jill had warned her.

She didn't think more about it as she watched. Other people stood near her, but Jill didn't take much note. Her sole focus was the man and the bull in the chute when Aaron nodded and the gate swung open wide.

Aaron's bull launched out of the chute. The animal's front end dropped low while his rear feet left the ground, reaching heights well over the heads of the bull fighters nearby.

Aaron's bull was the polar opposite of the flat bucker his friend had ridden in the last section. If Aaron could hang on, he'd get a hell of a score, and so far, he was.

He rocked against the bull's motion. He somehow managed to maintain his seat after each dip while at the same time fight the centrifugal force of the bull's fast spin.

The bull worked to dislodge him, yet still their movements meshed, like a dance between man and beast.

Jill couldn't take her eyes off the amazing sight, but time moved on and the eight-second buzzer sounded. Aaron reached down for the rope and Jill let herself breathe again when it released.

He flipped a leg over the bull's head and jumped off on the outside of the spin. Landing hard, he fell to his knees while the bull continued to buck deathly close. Aaron tucked his head beneath his arms, making himself a smaller target.

The bull's hooves struck the ground on either side of him. Bull fighters worked the whole time to distract the bull and draw it away from the downed rider. The moment the bull turned, Aaron scrambled away on all fours.

Finally, he stood upright and ran for the rails.

He was dirty but grinning when the announcer said, "Ninety points for Aaron Jordan. That puts him in second place for the night."

Confetti shot through the air as a cheer exploded from the crowd. One bull fighter high-fived Aaron before slapping him on the back with his other hand.

"What happened?" CeCe's voice behind her had Jill turning.

"Aaron got a ninety-point ride."

"Ninety out of what? One hundred? Is that good?"

The confetti littering the dirt and still hanging in the air should have answered CeCe's question, but Jill nodded. "Yes. It's very good. He's in second place."

"Oh. Well, that's wonderful."

True to his promise to CeCe, it wasn't more than a couple of minutes before Aaron was climbing the stairs to the VIP seating. That should make CeCe happy at least.

Aaron looked pretty happy as well. His wide smile showed how pleased he was with his ride.

Jill couldn't help her own smile. A ninety-point ride was always exciting, but actually knowing the guy who'd made it, even a little bit, made it even more so. "Aaron, that ride was amazing."

He dipped his head. "Thank you."

CeCe donned a brilliant smile. "Yes. Ninety points. Just amazing."

Jill drew back as her lying boss mimicked the compliment. CeCe hadn't even seen the ride, but Aaron didn't know that.

"Thank you much." He accepted the compliment before he leaned down to smack both legs of his jeans. A cloud of dust rose into the air. CeCe took a giant step back, away from Aaron. He cringed. "Sorry."

"Quite all right." For the first time that night, it looked as if she wasn't trying to be pressed up close against him.

Aaron must have noticed how CeCe still kept her distance. "I'd change into clean jeans, but I'm on the leaderboard. If that doesn't change I'll have to ride again in the short go."

CeCe raised her eyebrows and Jill knew she had no clue what Aaron meant as she said, "Of course."

Aaron might as well have been speaking Mandarin as far as CeCe was concerned.

"You're in second place and there's only a handful of riders left to ride. You'll make the short go." Jill's comment brought Aaron's attention around to her.

"Yeah, I know you're right. I just didn't wanna jinx it, you know?"

"Superstitious?" Jill asked.

"Little bit." Aaron grinned at her, which elicited a deep scowl from CeCe.

That not so subtle warning let Jill know she'd better keep any further commentary to herself.

CHAPTER SEVEN

"And Camo Cowboy bucks off Aaron Jordan at four-point-nine seconds."

Aaron heard the words reverberate through the arena.

With the wind knocked out of him from hitting the ground so hard, he didn't need the announcer's amplified recap bouncing off the walls to know he'd bucked off early.

He doubted any of the spectators needed that info either. They'd all heard that eight second buzzer sound while he lay on the ground gasping.

But that's what the announcers got paid the big bucks for. He supposed they had to do their job and state the obvious, even if it did make the buck off feel worse than it already did.

Thank God the bull fighters got the bull out of the arena fast, because Aaron wasn't sure he had it in him to scramble out of the animal's way had it chosen to come after him.

"You okay?"

Aaron squinted up into the lights and saw Wade Long, one of the bull fighters who'd saved his ass. "Yup. Just taking a little breather."

"That's what they all say." Wade laughed and extended his hand.

Aaron took it, grunting as the man hauled him off the ground. His ribs hurt. He was covered in dirt from head to toe, and all he wanted to do was have a few drinks with the boys and forget about the short go.

That's what he wanted to do. What he was required to do was go check in with Ms. Cole Shock Absorbers and see what she wanted to do.

Drawing in a breath that only made his ribcage hurt worse, Aaron grabbed the bull rope Wade handed him and hobbled his way toward the out gate.

It would be very nice to head directly back to the rider room and escape the cameramen intent on photographing his defeat, but he couldn't really do that either. Tom Parsons probably wouldn't like it. CeCe definitely wouldn't. Of that, Aaron was certain.

Weary, dirty and not up for playing host any longer, he climbed the stairs to the VIP seating.

"Hey, handsome." CeCe flashed him a brilliant smile, looking awfully upbeat considering he'd just wrecked. "So that's it, right? You're all done for the night?"

"Yup."

"So . . . what now?" CeCe's voice dropped suggestively low, as did her lids as she eyed him.

Thanks to his buck off in the short go, Aaron hadn't taken first place, so he didn't have to go down and smile for the cameras. The Brazilian who'd won was down there now doing exactly that. But Aaron had placed in the top three for the night, and that was pretty damn good in his opinion.

"I gotta sign autographs for the fans, but after that I'm done." Though not really done, since Tom expected Aaron to do whatever CeCe wanted.

She flashed him a smile of the whitest teeth he'd ever seen. "Good. Go sign your autographs and hurry back."

"I'll do my best." He turned toward the stairs, taking note that Jill was concentrating on her cell phone and pointedly ignoring that her boss's hand had been on his ass for the entire conversation.

What a fucked-up situation. Lucky for him, at the moment the cameras were more interested in the winner of the event than in what Aaron was doing with CeCe Cole. Hell. Aaron didn't know himself what he was doing with CeCe.

He headed down to the dirt where riders were lining up along the rails. He walked to the spot next to Skeeter and saw the black marker in his friend's hand.

Aaron let out a breath. "Crap. I got nothing to write with."

Some fans came armed with their own pens and permanent markers. Some didn't, which is why Aaron always remembered to grab his own—which was in his gear bag in the rider room, right where he'd forgotten it because CeCe had him so distracted.

"I got a spare." Skeeter pulled one out of his back pocket and handed it to Aaron.

"Thanks." Aaron let out a sigh.

Skeeter waved away the thanks. "No problem. Any time."

No problem for Skeeter. He wasn't the one who was so distracted he'd forget his head if it wasn't attached.

That was the end of the conversation and of Aaron reprimanding himself as the fans lined the rails and the riders started signing.

About fifteen minutes later, after they'd reached the last fan and autographed the final souvenir, Skeeter capped his marker. "That's it then."

"Yup." Aaron handed the marker in his hand back to Skeeter. "Thanks for that."

Skeeter took it and shoved both in his back pocket. "Anytime. So, Riley and I just gotta get the bulls settled for the night and then we'll meet you guys at the bar."

"I don't know if I can go."

A frown furrowed Skeeter's brow. "Why not?"

"Because I don't think my babysitting duty is done yet, and I don't want Tom Parsons pissed at me for ditching the sponsors."

Skeeter cringed. "That sucks."

"Yeah." Aaron nodded, though he had mixed feelings.

He could go out with the guys any night. It wasn't everyday he could do something like this for the head of the association. If he did it well, it could maybe help his career. It sure couldn't hurt to have Tom owe him a favor.

Of course, Aaron didn't know what to feel if it ended up that what CeCe wanted was to get sweaty with him.

Glancing up, he saw her smiling down at him with the same hungry expression he'd seen all night whenever she looked at him.

Sleeping with the sponsor seemed like a really bad idea. But from what little he knew of CeCe after spending the past few hours with her, refusing her could be much worse.

CeCe Cole didn't strike him as the kind of woman who liked to be told *no*.

Garret ambled over with Chase behind him. "You ready to go?"

"Not sure I can. I gotta see what CeCe's doing now." Aaron repeated the excuse, but Garret didn't give him the same reaction as Skeeter.

Instead, his brother-in-law grinned. "All right. Have fun."

Aaron snorted out a wordless response at that. Anxious to get away before there were any more questions or comments from the guys, Aaron made a break for it. He took the stairs fast, which put him in front of CeCe in a matter of seconds.

He glanced around and noticed she was alone. "Where's Jill?"

CeCe took a step forward until they were almost touching. She was tall. In her heels, and with her standing so close, she was eye level with him.

"I sent her back to the hotel. She has work to do and I want you all to myself." CeCe ran a single perfectly manicured nail down his arm, sending a shiver through him.

Aaron swallowed hard. "Oh. Okay."

"So are you ready to go?"

"Uh, yup." Ready to go where, was the question uppermost in Aaron's mind, but he couldn't bring himself to ask it. Judging by the hungry look she leveled on him, he had a feeling he knew what she wanted to do when they got there. "I just have to get my gear bag from the rider room. And I gotta grab my truck keys."

"Leave your truck here. We're taking my limo."

Her limo. The night got a little more surreal.

Apparently, Aaron didn't need to know where they were headed since he wasn't driving. He also would be stuck wherever she brought him since he wouldn't have a vehicle, but he wasn't about to argue.

"All right." Aaron swept his arm before them. "Ladies first."

She was leading him around like a puppy on a leash anyway. He figured he should at least pretend something about tonight was his idea and at the same time be a gentleman by letting her go ahead.

"Thank you." CeCe treated him to another sultry smile and started down the stairs.

At the bottom, Aaron noticed Garret watching them. His brother-in-law flashed a thumbs up. Aaron rolled his eyes. He needed to get her into the limo before Garret did anything to embarrass him.

With a hand on the small of her back, he led CeCe down the hallway, pausing just outside the dressing room. "I'll be back in a sec. Stay right here."

"Why? Are there a bunch of naked cowboys inside?" She leaned around him, trying to see.

"Could be." He nodded. "And a whole lot of cussing not fit for a lady."

She leaned in close to his ear. "Later, I'll show you how many cuss words I know and how much of a lady I am . . . or am not."

He swallowed hard. "Okay, I'll be right back."

Aaron escaped through the doorway to the sound of CeCe's laughter. He crossed the crowded room and made a beeline for the bench where he'd left his bag, avoiding eye contact with anyone.

He didn't need any riders asking questions any more than

he wanted to have to provide answers.

One quick glance told him Garret, Skeeter and Chase weren't in the room. They were probably huddled together somewhere discussing him. He couldn't worry about them now. He had far bigger things to worry about. Such as how he was going with CeCe in her limo probably to her hotel where she was going to prove to him she wasn't a lady.

Shit.

Bag in hand, Aaron headed out the door and found CeCe right where he'd left her.

"Ready?" she asked.

Not even close.

He held up his bag. "Yup."

"Good. The limo is out front waiting."

Out front where the fans exited the building. There was no way they wouldn't see Aaron getting into CeCe's limo.

Perhaps that was the point. She wanted to be seen leaving with him. He should be grateful, not worried. Of all the riders, CeCe Cole had chosen to be seen leaving with him.

More than a few men they passed took a second look as CeCe strutted by. He shot her a sideways glance and saw the sexy pout on her lips. She had to walk in front of him to get through the door and his gaze dropped to the sway of her hips as she walked.

There was no doubt about it. CeCe Cole was an attractive woman. Drop dead gorgeous, in fact. Maybe it was about time Aaron stopped thinking so damn hard and just enjoyed this night.

As he tipped his hat lower over his face to try and avoid being noticed leaving with CeCe he realized that might be easier said than done.

CHAPTER EIGHT

The limo driver opened the door and CeCe paused to address him. "The hotel. And put up the privacy shield."

She slid in, leaving Aaron on the sidewalk with his pulse racing.

At least now he knew where they were going. He ducked into the car behind her. After tossing his bag on the opposite seat, he settled next to CeCe.

The driver slammed the door. Seconds later, the privacy shield rose. So did Aaron's heart rate.

CeCe stretched one long leg over his and leaned closer, running her hand up his chest. "Don't be nervous, sweetie."

"I'm not nervous." The high pitch of his reply didn't sound very convincing to him. He could only imagine what it sounded like to her.

She leaned closer. "I can feel your heart pounding through your shirt. You're not a virgin, are you?"

"No. Of course not." He couldn't be insulted by the question since he was acting like one.

"Good." That was the last thing she said before her mouth covered his.

While locked at the lips, she moved to straddle him, and

any lingering doubt he'd been irrationally holding on to fled. There was no longer any question that CeCe wanted much more from him than a tour of the arena.

She reached for his belt, undoing the buckle surprisingly fast considering she was working blind while she kissed him. She made short work of the button on his fly and then went for his zipper.

As she eased it down, Aaron's mind whirled. Sex in a limo with the tour's biggest sponsor. It was crazy.

Even so, he was hard as a rock, a fact CeCe didn't miss as she slipped her hand inside his underwear. "Mmm. Nice."

"CeCe, we can't do this here."

"Why not?" She grasped his length.

Aaron sucked in a breath as she pulled him free of his underwear. He couldn't think with her stroking him. He stilled her hand with his and forced his mind back to the situation.

For one, not having all that much experience with limousines, he didn't totally believe the privacy glass was all that private. A more pressing matter was the fact the condom stash he always carried was divided between his truck and the suitcase in his hotel room, meaning he had nothing with him now.

That seemed like a good place to start. "No condoms."

"That's easily remedied." She smiled and reached for the phone he hadn't noticed before. "Driver, I need you to stop at the next store you see and pick up a box of condoms."

As Aaron sat shocked into silence during this crazy phone conversation between CeCe and the limo driver, she glanced down at his exposed erection. She shook her had and said, "Regular size should be fine."

Jesus, if this guy decided to sell this story to a tabloid, not only would everyone in the world—his parents included—know he'd been having sex with CeCe Cole in a limo, but they'd also know he didn't need the extra-large condoms. Great.

When she hung up the phone, Aaron knocked himself out

of his shock. "CeCe, he could tell somebody."

She shrugged. "So?"

Aaron wasn't a huge celebrity, but she kind of was. Besides, in the day of social media, it wasn't necessary for the media to publish a story for it to spread like wildfire. Even the driver casually posting on his Facebook about his client's request could be enough to have the story go viral.

"So? Don't you care that he could tell everyone what we're doing back here?" Aaron kept his voice low, still afraid the driver could hear everything.

"I hope he does. I want my bastard ex-husband to know exactly how much fun I'm having now that he's gone."

"But—"

"I do love that you're such a boy scout." She ran her fingernail up his erection, which had started to fade during the conversation. "Let me see if I can help you relax a little, shall I?"

He didn't have time to argue before she slid her mouth over his cock. A shudder ran through him as she took him all in, surrounding him with wet heat.

The car came to a stop and he heard the driver's door slam. Relieved they were finally alone in the car, he closed his eyes and leaned his head back. He couldn't fight her expert effort any more than he could deny he was starting to not care about where they were.

"Do you know why my ex-husband and I divorced?" She had slid off him long enough to ask the question, before the heat of her mouth engulfed him again.

"No." His single word came out on a breath.

She lifted her head again and focused her eyes on his. "I wasn't enough for him. Am I enough for you, Aaron?"

"Yes, ma'am." More than enough. A little too much, truth be told.

His body tightened. If she kept up what she was doing, he'd come and there'd be no need for those condoms in the immediate future.

She smiled. "I think we're going to have a lovely weekend

together."

"Weekend?" A whole weekend with this woman might just kill him.

"I have no other plans. Do you?" she asked.

"No, ma'am."

"Good." A knock on the car window had her glancing up at him. "Get that, will you?"

His eyes flew open as she slid her lush lips over his length again, taking him all the way in until he hit the back of her throat. He evaluated the situation and decided the only course of action was to open the window an inch or two and hope the driver couldn't see in.

He hit the button. Stopping the window after it opened just a crack, Aaron asked. "Yes?"

"I have the items you requested." There was no amusement in the driver's voice, though Aaron was sure this would be the topic of discussion after the guy's shift was up.

"Can you shove them through the crack?"

"You need to lower the window more."

If CeCe would just sit up and stop what she was doing, he would do that gladly. He was going to suggest that as she reached out, mouth still on his cock, and pushed the button to lower the window more than half way.

Mortified, Aaron tried to sit up straighter. Tried to look like he wasn't buried balls deep in this woman's mouth. He was pretty sure he failed.

A paper bag came at him through the open window. He grabbed it and scrambled for the button. Willing the window to rise faster, he blurted, "Thank you."

"My pleasure." This time Aaron heard the amusement in the driver's voice and his humiliation grew.

"About time." CeCe chose that moment to sit up, reaching for the bag Aaron had in his hand. She tore into the box, pulled out a strip and tossed the rest to the side.

Using her perfect teeth, she ripped the wrapper. Then she was covering him while he sat by, not helping, but not stopping her either.

With his cock hard and ready, he had to think he wasn't as opposed to sex in the back of the limo as he'd first thought. She tugged her lace underwear down her legs and tossed them onto the opposite seat. He watched as they landed on his gear bag.

CeCe lifted her skirt and straddled him again. This time there was nothing separating them save the latex. She lowered herself over him and he was done worrying.

He hissed in a breath. "God, you're so tight."

"I'll pass the compliment along to my doctor."

"What?" He frowned, barely comprehending what she'd said as he filled her tight heat.

"Search vaginal rejuvenation online one day. Now *shh*. Enough questions, boy scout."

"I'm not a boy scout." Her name for him was beginning to feel like an insult.

"Prove it."

He was buried deep inside the tour sponsor and at least one person, the limo driver, knew what was happening. He'd either get in trouble for what they were doing or he wouldn't. Either way, it was too late now. There was nothing more to do except go with it.

Enough acting like the boy she accused him of being. Time to show her he was a man.

"Fine. I will." He flipped her onto her back on the seat and followed her down.

Aaron lifted her hips and thrust deep, forcing a breath from her.

He set a fast pace, taking satisfaction as she closed her eyes and matched each one of his strokes with a loud cry.

No longer worrying about the soundproofing in the back of the car, he smiled when she cried out louder.

CeCe clutched at his arms and he felt her body tighten around his.

She could call him boy scout all she wanted, but he'd show her exactly how much he knew about being a man. If that partition wasn't soundproof, he'd prove it to the driver as well.

This part, where Aaron made CeCe come until she screamed, had better make it into the driver's retelling of the tale.

Determined, he kept going. Hell, when he set his mind to it, he could go on as long as she could.

Hopefully, the hotel wasn't too close. If it was? Well, then the driver had better circle a few times. He wasn't going to have CeCe Cole walk away and say Aaron Jordan hadn't given her the ride of a lifetime.

CHAPTER NINE

The arena had emptied of spectators and the parking lot was nearly deserted of vehicles.

Jill pulled out her cell phone and checked the time.

Maybe she'd missed the cab by standing inside the glass doors of the building in the air conditioning rather than outside? But she hadn't taken her eyes off the spot out front where she'd told the taxi to meet her. She'd have seen any car pull up.

"Dammit."

"Problem?" A male voice had Jill turning.

She saw a guy about her own age standing behind her. After a closer look she realized he was familiar to her because she'd seen Aaron talking to him during the event. He was one of the riders who'd competed, but at the moment she couldn't come up with his name.

"I called a cab about forty-five minutes ago and it never came."

He cringed. "I doubt a taxi is going to be happy to come all the way out here to the arena."

Jill scowled. "Great."

"Where you headed?"

"My hotel." As she answered, Jill noticed the wedding band tattooed on his ring finger.

This guy was not only married, he was so in love and sure he'd never get a divorce, he'd actually had his ring tattooed on.

Story of her life. Most of the cute ones were taken, and the single one CeCe had scooped up for herself.

"Narrow that down a little bit and I'll see if I can hook you up with a ride." The mystery rider smiled. "Which hotel?"

"The Mandarin in Buckhead."

"The Mandarin? *Pfft*. Yeah, none of us guys are staying there. First off, we can't afford it with the prices they charge. And second, that's like half an hour away. We're at the Garden Inn. Seventy-nine dollars a night, Wi-Fi, HBO and free breakfast." The dark-haired guy grinned. "I'm Garret, by the way."

Garret. That jogged her memory. She'd seen his name on the roster. "Jill."

"Yeah, I know. The Cole Shock Absorbers marketing chick."

She laughed at his description. "Yup. How did you know that?"

"Aaron told me. He's my brother-in-law. And actually, since Silver and I had our baby, he's now also Uncle Aaron to my son."

After getting over the surprise that Aaron had taken the time to mention her to his brother-on-law, Jill pawed through her knowledge of the rider roster. She remembered seeing that Garret James had married Aaron Jordan's sister a year, maybe closer to two years ago.

"I'd take you over to the hotel myself, but I didn't drive here."

"That's okay. I'll just try calling the cab again or try a different company."

He glanced at the readout on his phone. "You know, if I call my friends and tell them I'm gonna be late meeting them at the bar I can run you to the Mandarin quick if you want. Unless . . . if you don't have to get right back, do you wanna come out? It's just gonna be a bunch of us grabbing some hot wings and a couple of beers."

Drowning the memory of this night seemed pretty good to her. "Hot wings and beer sound really good about now."

She had the shots from the photographer waiting for her, but she could do that in the morning while CeCe was sleeping in. The woman never had been an early riser.

"Great. Who knows, maybe while hanging out with us you'll find something to use for your job."

"Oh really? While drinking beer and eating hot wings?"

He grinned. "Not the beer and wings part, but you'll be surrounded by riders, stock contractors, and sometimes a bull fighter or two will show up. Since Cole is a sponsor of the tour, that might be useful."

"So you're saying I can call it work and write tonight off on my expense report?"

Garret laughed. "Hell yeah. If I had an expense report, I'd totally do that. Come on. I've got Chase's truck. He went with Riley and Skeeter to help with the bulls."

"Thanks." She matched his stride as they made their way down the steps.

"No problem. I figure you could use a drink."

Jill looked at Garret. "Why is that?"

"Ms. Shock Absorber looks like she can be a handful." Garret shot her a sideways glance when she didn't answer. "But I know you can't speak ill of your boss."

Jill longed to agree, but professionalism wouldn't allow her to do that. "It has been a long day . . . and night."

"Yeah, I figured." He grinned at her small concession. Garret halted at a truck and frowned.

"Is this your friend's?"

"No, actually this is Aaron's truck. I guess he got a ride to . . . wherever." Garret cleared his throat and hooked a thumb toward the next row. "Mine is right over there. Come on."

With a hand on her back, it felt as if Garret were rushing

her away from the scene of a crime. As if he wanted to protect her from what she had already figured out—that CeCe had taken Aaron in the limo, which is why she'd told Jill to take a cab to the hotel.

Perhaps Jill should stop worrying and enjoy a CeCe-free, not to mention a drama-free night.

After she climbed into the passenger seat of the truck Garret had opened the door of, she slipped the strap of her purse off her shoulder. Her bag contained her corporate credit card. Given the inconvenience of CeCe taking the limo and leaving Jill stranded, she figured she was justified in taking advantage of her expense account.

Maybe she'd even buy the riders a round or two. That seemed like the least a big sponsor like Cole could do.

Garret James ran around to the other side of the truck. Jill waited for him to be settled behind the wheel, his keys in the ignition, the big engine rumbling beneath them before she broached the topic of the elephant in the room—or in the cab of the truck, as the case may be. "Garret, we don't have to pretend."

He glanced at her from the driver's seat. "Pretend about what?"

"I know Aaron left with my boss." In the limo, leaving Jill stranded with no ride in a land without taxis, apparently.

Thank goodness for the kindness of strangers . . . and Aaron's brother-in-law.

"Well, you know, he was supposed to play tour guide for her so they uh, probably went sightseeing."

"Yeah, I'm sure that's it . . . If the sights are in her hotel room." She mumbled the last part beneath her breath, but Garret's burst of a laugh told her he'd heard.

Grinning, he glanced her direction before concentrating back on the road. "You said it, not me."

"Me? I didn't say a word." Jill feigned ignorance.

Garret laughed. "Gotcha."

Jill knew the deal. This wasn't her first experience traveling with CeCe since the divorce had been finalized and the former Mrs. Cole was free to do what she pleased. She also knew better than to comment on it. That kind of curtailed the conversation in the cab of the truck for the drive to the bar.

"And we're here," Garret announced.

"Really? Already?" The trip was shorter than she'd expected, even with the awkward lack of conversation in the truck.

"Yup. There's the bar. And that there next door is the riders' hotel. Not quite as fancy as yours but we like to keep things close by. We travel so much to the events, once we're in town, the less driving we have to do the better."

Jill glanced at the hotel directly next to the bar. "Don't worry. I won't ask you drive me to my hotel later after you've been drinking. I can just call a cab from here."

Garret glanced at her as he put the truck into park and cut the ignition. "I might just let you. After that buck off I had, I was hoping to have a few to drown the pain, if you really would be okay in a taxi. We're in town here. There should be plenty of cabs who'll come get you."

"I'm sure the bartender has a list. I'll be fine. Thanks for the ride here and the invite."

"No problem." He reached for the door handle on his side. "I saw the stock trailer parked across the street, so Riley, Skeeter and Chase must be here already too."

"Cool." Jill let herself out of the truck, hopping down from the high vehicle.

She had to admit that hanging with riders and stock contractors at a bar after the event sounded like it was going to be pretty fun. She'd never get this behind-the-scenes look elsewhere.

Speaking of looks—she was getting quite of few of them from the table that Garret led her to inside. "Hey, guys. This is Jill."

The wide-eyed stares she and Garret were getting from his friends had Jill rushing to explain. "I work for Cole Shock Absorbers. I was waiting for a cab at the arena. It never came so Garret was nice enough to offer me a ride."

"And now I'm going to go get us something to drink. Beer? Something else?" he asked her.

"Beer is great. Thanks."

Garret nodded and turned for the bar.

"I thought I recognized you," a young blond rider said. "You were up in the chute seats with Aaron."

It was amazing he had seen her at all, considering CeCe was there too. Jill tended to not get noticed when her boss was around.

"I was." She nodded.

"Since Garret didn't bother to introduce us . . ." The rider stood and extended his hand. "I'm Chase Reese. This is Skeeter Anderson and that's Riley Davis."

Skeeter and Riley smiled and said hello and Jill had to think this could be the nicest group of people she'd met in a long time. Then again, that was no surprise considering she'd been hanging around CeCe. The difference between genuine, down to earth people and a self centered, rich, bitter divorcee was pretty glaring.

Garret arrived back with their two beers and she thanked him and gladly took a gulp.

"So where'd you leave Aaron?" Skeeter asked.

"I didn't leave him anywhere. He and CeCe left me, actually." Jill hadn't even finished one whole beer and she was already speaking out of turn. She'd better bite her tongue.

Skeeter grinned. "Got it."

Riley backhanded Skeeter's leg. "Don't gossip. You don't know what they're doing."

Jill couldn't help the snort that escaped her. When she glanced up, she noticed the group watching her. "Sorry. You're right. We don't know what they're doing. So, I heard you guys are stock contractors?"

Skeeter nodded. "Riley owns the best bucking bulls in the country."

Jill's widened her eyes. "That's impressive."

The girl didn't look old enough to drink. Since she was sipping on a soda, maybe she wasn't.

"And I wouldn't be able to keep them if it wasn't for your help." Riley sent a puppy dog look in Skeeter's direction.

Garret leaned in, as if to confide in Jill. "You have to forgive these two. They're in love."

Chase raised a brow at his fellow rider. "Don't you tease them. You're just as bad with Silver and that baby of yours—you'd hang the moon for that kid."

"That I would." Garret checked his phone. "Damn. I was gonna call but they're probably asleep already. And you should talk, Chase. When Leesa's around you're no better than the rest of us."

"I know. Wait until I convince her to marry me and start working on a baby of our own." He grinned.

Jill watched the conversation. "So is Aaron the only one who's single?"

Garret nodded. "Of us guys, yeah. As for the other riders, Slade is married. Mustang might as well be. The two Aussies are married now. The Brazilians are mostly married too."

"There are a couple of the really young ones who are single. But they're like eighteen," Skeeter said.

Chase blew out a breath. "One's seventeen, I think. They started real young."

"About as young as Skeeter here." Garret shot his friend a grin.

"Jealous, old man?" Skeeter cocked a brow and teased, but Jill didn't think he was serious. Garret didn't look like he was even thirty yet. Though in this sport, thirty was old.

"A little jealous maybe." Garret laughed. "So anyway, yeah. Most of us are taken. You looking for boyfriend?"

Chase's gaze joined Garret's on her as he said, "I think there's a new young Canadian rider who's single if you want an introduction."

Jill had to nip this in the bud. "Thanks, but no. I was just curious. I'm not looking for a bull rider boyfriend."

"Smart girl." Garret raised his beer to her in a toast.

It was interesting, though, how the head of the organization had specifically chosen Aaron, one of the few single riders at this event, to play host to CeCe.

Very interesting indeed.

Perhaps her boss's reputation with men had proceeded her? Or perhaps Jill should stop worrying and enjoy her night off. With that in mind, she downed a good portion of her beer.

Standing, she grabbed her purse. She had very few perks at this job. An expense account and corporate credit card for travel was one of them. The least she could do was pay back the kindness of the riders who were part of the association Cole's Shocks gave so much money to sponsor.

"What's everybody drinking? Next round is on Cole Shock Absorbers."

Judging by the smiles of those around the table, that offer had scored her some brownie points. After working in CeCe's shadow since the divorce, Jill would take all the goodwill she could get.

CHAPTER TEN

"Nice room." Aaron took in the sprawling space.

Glancing around, he realized that calling it a room had been a gross understatement. It would be more accurate to call it a suite. One outfitted with a seating area and large-screen television on one side and what looked like a kitchen and dining area on the other.

CeCe ignored Aaron's comment and headed across the living room. She paused in a doorway to what must be her bedroom, judging by the sprawling mattress he could see just a bit past her.

She cocked up one of her perfectly shaped brows. "What are you waiting for?"

A drink? Some conversation? Something other than her unspoken order to get in her bed. Then again, they'd already had sex in the limo, while the driver was in the damn car, so he probably shouldn't expect verbal foreplay or any other niceties at this point.

He followed her path across the room and stopped where she stood. She reached out and fingered the snaps on his riding shirt. She popped one open. "I want you naked."

Yup, no delusions here. No games either. They were doing

this. Again.

He should be happy. He'd gotten laid once already tonight and by all indications was about to again, all without any effort on his part. She walked across the bedroom, kicking off her shoes with each step before she dropped her dress to the floor.

Super model CeCe Cole naked was not a bad thing. He got a good look at her now—all of her—as she stretched out on the king-sized bed. She spread her long, lean legs and gave Aaron a clear view of everything she had to offer.

Nothing about this was what he'd expected, but that wouldn't stop him from enjoying the situation. Aaron strode forward and moved to crawl between her legs.

CeCe shook her head. "Nuh, uh. I said I want you naked."

She was right. He'd never gotten a chance to change. Even with as much as he'd tried to knock off any dirt, he was still in the clothes he'd ridden—and wrecked in. He was too covered in dust to be on her bed.

Standing, he toed off his boots while pulling off the shirt. After working on his buckle, he glanced up to see CeCe's stare glued to his bare torso.

Maybe her request wasn't based on her worry about dirt getting on her bed after all. She had the look of a woman who was hungry, and not for food.

Women weren't usually this attentive while he got undressed.

Lowering the zipper of his fly, he watched her as she watched him. He hadn't been to many strip clubs—the drinks cost too damn much to go often—but he'd been to enough to know he should take his time to build the suspense for her.

He wasn't disappointed by her reaction to his striptease. When he pushed his jeans down, her gaze shot to the bulge tenting his briefs. At the sight of it, she actually licked her lips.

That sped along his little show. He abandoned the underwear and crawled on to the bed.

CeCe scooted herself all the way up the mattress to the

headboard. Rolling on her side, she crooked one finger and beckoned to him. "Come on up here, lover boy."

Lover boy? He'd take that. Hell, he'd been called worse, by her in fact.

Smiling at the potential of what he could do in a bed this size, Aaron crawled toward her. When he'd reached her, she said, "On your back."

"Okay." He did as told.

Apparently, she was the kind of woman who liked to be in charge. In business. In bed. Whatever. Lying on his back, he figured letting the woman take control was just fine with him once in a while.

CeCe moved to straddle him. He was going to remind her that he'd left the box of condoms in his gear bag, when she said, "Arms up above your head."

"What?" He frowned as she reached toward the nightstand and opened the drawer. She pulled out two long scarves. When she ignored his question and proceeded to tie the end of each scarf to the headboard, he felt compelled to ask it again. "Wait. What are you doing?"

"Tying you up." She spoke as she took his wrist and wrapped the end of one scarf around it.

CeCe reached for his other wrist and he started to panic. "Why?"

He wouldn't exactly call it claustrophobia, but he wasn't real big on feeling confined, as in he liked to have free use of his hands, thank you very much.

"I like to play with my food before I eat it." She raked her heavily lidded gaze down his body.

He started to get an inkling of what she had in mind. He couldn't know exactly what she meant, but he could guess. If it involved her mouth on his dick again, he was okay with having his hands tied. "All right. But just so you know, I'm pretty dang good with my hands, so you might want to let me use them at some point during this."

She shook her head at his attempt at levity. "Not yet. Later. I'm more interested in other parts of you at the moment."

CeCe moved down the bed, and down his body, dragging his attention away from the fact he was tied up as he anticipated what would come next. She slid her hands along his torso. His body tightened just from his thinking about her mouth surrounding him again.

He stared at her lips, so full and lush. He'd never seen a woman in real life with such plump lips. In the movies, yes, but never on one who was slipping his cock between them. He was no virgin, but he could swear he trembled with anticipation as she leaned lower.

"Bend your knees, lover boy."

He did as she requested, widening his legs at the same time to give her plenty of room. He'd do anything she wanted, as long as she wrapped that hot mouth around him again.

Mesmerized, he watched her slide one finger between her lips. The woman knew how to tease. The move ramped up his need to a whole other level.

After pulling the finger out of her mouth ever so slowly, she smiled. She reached for him, running that finger over the oh-so-sensitive head of his cock.

The mind was a powerful thing. His imagination had his body already reacting and she'd barely touched him.

CeCe ran her finger down his length and continued lower. He let his eyes drift shut. It was torture, but the best kind. She palmed the weight of his balls in one hand while teasing him with that single finger. She moved her hand beneath him and continued even lower.

Too low.

He jumped, opening his eyes as she reached a spot he didn't think she needed to be touching. Thinking that maybe it was an accident, he pulled his pelvis away from her hand, pressing harder into the mattress, trying to get out of range of her probing finger.

With his hands tied, there wasn't much more he could do besides kick her in the face, and he wasn't panicked enough to do that.

"Stay still." She moved with him. Keeping her finger right where it was in spite of his efforts she circled his tight hole.

Clenching both his butt and his jaw, he asked, "What are you doing?"

"You'll see soon enough."

There was a beautiful naked woman touching him. Theoretically, he should let her do whatever the hell she wanted. But this . . . this was an area he had no experience in, and he wasn't sure he wanted any.

He tried to reason this out and keep himself calm. If all she continued to do was this unwelcome but not entirely unpleasant massage, he could deal with it.

"Relax."

Easy for her to say.

Trying to keep from looking like a nervous boy, he decided to make a joke. "Maybe there's something you could do to help me relax."

She smiled. "Maybe there is."

CeCe leaned down and then the heat of her mouth, which he remembered so well from the limo, surrounded him. He let out a breath tinged with a moan.

Closing his eyes, he pressed his head back into the pillow and settled in for an amazing ride. She worked him with her mouth with long slow strokes. Tantalizing him until he started to enjoy the combination of her mouth and her touch.

He should have trusted her from the beginning. From what he could tell, she knew how to please a man. She should. She must have had lots of practice. After all, she'd been married.

Just the tip of her finger poked inside him. Very happy to be buried deep in her mouth, he breathed through the panic. The gentle probing in time with the stroke of the mouth covering him set a rhythm he got used to quickly enough.

As disturbing as the invasion had been, he wasn't a man who got blowjobs often enough to even think of stopping her during this one. Her obsession with his ass aside, the woman was amazingly good at what she was doing to his cock.

He felt her push her finger deeper, slow but with enough pressure he knew she wasn't stopping.

"CeCe." He yanked his hips up to get away from the finger that felt as if it was completely inside him.

"Trust me. Just relax."

There was no way he could do either of those things. She wasn't even sucking him off now. She'd abandoned that in favor of concentrating all of her energy on invading his body with more enthusasm than before.

"CeCe, please—" His plea was cut off as she hit a spot with her finger that sent a near electrical charge through him.

She smiled and lowered her mouth over him again. Aaron groaned from the combination of the two sensations, bowing his spine off the bed. She stroked up and down, using hand and mouth until he was straining against the scarves binding him to the headboard.

It wasn't long before he felt his body tightening, getting closer to release. CeCe lifted her head. His cock popped out of her mouth, standing straight up on its own.

The steady press and release of her finger inside him didn't stop. Neither did the tingling building within him as he came closer to losing control.

She gripped his shaft with one hand and continued to work him inside with the other. "Don't you dare come."

He opened his eyes wide at her order. There was no way he could hold back. He opened his mouth to tell her but all that came out was a groan. The orgasm broke over him. Helpless to stop it, he watched each spurt arc into the air in time with every press of her finger.

The pleasure went on forever. At least, that's what it felt like. Even after she'd drained him of all he had, he continued to come. Dry pulses that left him weak and breathless, until he was gasping. Boneless.

When his body could take no more and he shrunk to a shadow of his former self in her hand, she stopped the torturous pleasure.

He hissed in a breath as she yanked her finger out of him too fast. Things were tender down there. As happy as he was that she was finally done, he'd wanted her to be slow and gentle in her retreat. She wasn't, but he wasn't going to complain. Not while his hands were still tied and she was so obviously in control of things. Delicate things.

"I bet the girls you're used to don't make you feel like that. Do they?" Her hand remained on his slack cock as she talked.

If she was hoping for him to get hard after that, she was going to have to wait a while. And get him some water so he could rehydrate.

"Nope." He could honestly say not another living soul had ever had him in this position in his life. Even if it hadn't been true, there was no way he was telling CeCe that. His family jewels were at her mercy.

Looking satisfied, she finally released her hold on him and sat up on her knees.

She smiled. "You are absolutely adorable."

"Thanks. You, uh, going to undo these?" He glanced at the scarves holding his arms hostage and making his hands go numb.

"Eventually." Still straddling him, CeCe moved farther up his body until she was sitting on his chest.

He felt the heat between her thighs against his skin, but it wasn't enough to get him aroused again so soon. If that was what she was hoping for, she was out of luck. He had to tilt his head back to look up at her face.

"So how are you with your mouth?" she asked.

His eyes popped wide as he realized what she was asking. "Uh, pretty good. I guess."

"Excellent." Grabbing the headboard, CeCe rose above him, and then he was no longer looking at her face.

She lowered herself over his mouth and Aaron began to realize it didn't matter to her whether he could get hard again right away or not. She obviously had other plans.

CHAPTER ELEVEN

Jill pulled off her glasses and rubbed a hand over her closed lids.

Her eyes hurt. She'd opted for her glasses rather than her contact lenses, but even so, staring at tiny thumbnails of photos on her computer screen for the past couple of hours was starting to get to her.

It was the only way to quickly scroll through them all. She had to choose which ones would go on the company blog and which would be in the email newsletter. There were some others she'd post on the company's social media pages. Then there were the few unflattering shots where CeCe looked bad. There weren't many, but those that did exist had to be deleted before CeCe saw them or Jill would have to hear about it.

Jill sighed and put her glasses back on. Damn. She needed coffee. She needed more sleep too, but she wanted to get this done before CeCe woke up. Not that she had to rush. The woman could easily sleep until noon.

What Jill really needed was some pain reliever to kill the dull ache in her head caused by too much beer, too little food and the ill-advised rounds of shots at the bar last night.

She stood and moved to the door that connected her room to the living area of CeCe's suite. There hadn't been any noise coming out of the suite this morning, so she must be still sleeping. There was no reason to suffer with the tiny coffee maker and powdered creamer in her own room when CeCe had a stocked fridge and a full-sized coffee maker.

The lure of fresh coffee and real cream gave Jill the incentive to brave pushing the door open. She peered through the crack along the doorframe. The coast was clear, so she moved into the room, padding softly to the kitchen area.

CeCe would be pissed if she didn't have a pot of coffee brewed for her whenever she woke, so Jill really did have a good excuse to be there, even if it was for herself.

As silently as possible, she filled the filter with grounds and the carafe with water. A push of a button and blessed hot coffee was on the way.

As the coffee brewed, Jill opened the fridge. While she reached for the cream, she spotted the English muffins on the shelf and below them the melon and fresh berries.

Darn it. Now she was really hungry.

She grabbed the container of cream and a strawberry, deciding to make do with that. She could always order room service and have a real breakfast delivered to her own room. Eggs Benedict would be darn good right about now, and the perfect way to soothe her still tired and hung over body.

Jill was just popping the strawberry into her mouth while elbowing the door shut when she turned and smothered a scream.

Aaron, looking half asleep, not to mention almost naked, held up his hands. "Sorry. Sorry. I didn't realize you were here."

She pulled the strawberry back out of her mouth. "No, it's my fault. I didn't realize you were here."

Or rather still here, because Jill had been pretty certain when they'd found Aaron's truck abandoned at the arena that CeCe had dragged him back with her. She just hadn't thought

CeCe would have kept him there all night.

"I don't have my truck. I couldn't leave. I called Garret last night but it was late and—"

"He was too drunk to come get you," Jill finished his sentence.

Yeah, that first round of shots had been her doing. So had the second one. She'd gotten pretty loose with the company credit card last night, if she remembered correctly. Of course, drinks in that place had been so ridiculously cheap she hadn't done all that much damage. Even after she'd paid for the taxi to take her from the bar to the hotel.

"Yeah, he was pretty drunk. Chase too." Aaron frowned. "How do you know?"

That's what he was worried about? How she knew his friends had been drunk? He should probably be more concerned that he was standing in front of her in nothing but navy blue briefs that didn't hide a whole lot of anything.

Worse, Jill hadn't had sex with a man in so long she wasn't at all offended at his state of undress.

In fact, she was more interested in catching a glimpse of the tantalizing outline within those briefs. Was that a raging morning hard-on he was sporting or was the man just naturally that big?

She yanked her eyes and her mind off Aaron's assets and tried to remember the question. "Um, I was out with them last night at the bar."

He lifted his brows. "You were?"

"Uh huh. I was."

She had to turn away, because the sight of his bare chest was waking up body parts she would rather remain in hibernation.

If this man was going to be CeCe's boy toy of choice for the duration of their stay, it was pointless for Jill to fantasize about what it would feel like to run her hands over those rock-hard abs. Or how it would be to trace her fingers along that happy trail of fine hair that led downward.

She pulled her focus up to his incredible eyes, which only

had her imagining staring into them as he looked up at her from between her legs while he—

Grabbing the coffee carafe, she turned toward him. "Coffee?" Jill cleared her throat of the husky, sex-fantasy tone she heard in it.

"Yeah, eventually. Is there any cold water? I'm really thirsty and the water out of the bathroom tap tastes like crap."

"There's a whole case of bottles in the fridge." Jill should know. She had to buy them and put them there or endure CeCe's bitching.

"Thanks."

The sound of the refrigerator door opening had Jill pausing as she poured her coffee long enough to glance over her shoulder and get a look at the muscles of his broad back that narrowed in a vee at his waist.

Then there were those tight ass cheeks beneath the soft navy cotton. Damn. She forced her attention back to getting the hot coffee into the cup before she spilled it.

Frigging CeCe. How selfish was she, grabbing him all for herself? Aaron was half CeCe's age. She should be looking for her next husband, or at least a man her own age. Not scooping up one of the few single riders on the tour—not to mention the hottest one—and holding him hostage in her hotel room.

"You know, you could have called the limo to take you to your truck anytime you wanted."

Of course, maybe he hadn't wanted to leave all that badly. He'd called his friends, yes, but the disheveled state of his hair and the sleep-deprived look on his face told Jill he'd been busy doing something all night long. And most likely not sleeping.

He drew his brows low. "I didn't realize I could do that."

"Yup. The front desk or the concierge would have called the car for you. The driver's on call twenty-four hours a day." CeCe wouldn't have had it any other way. When Jill glanced up from stirring cream and sugar into her coffee, she noticed

Aaron's cheeks looking flushed.

He finally shot her a glance. "I'm not sure I want to see him again. The limo driver, I mean."

Jill lifted her brows. "Oh."

Nothing left to say to that. Not a surprise really that CeCe would have started the amorous activities in the limo. She was an exhibitionist, to say the least.

Jill would have to remember to give the driver an extra big tip for having to endure whatever CeCe had put him through. Maybe it would help keep the man's mouth shut about whatever he'd seen or heard.

With a definite lag in the conversation and nothing better to do, Jill reached for the strawberry she'd abandoned on the counter and took a bite. Aaron's eyes tracked the motion, remaining on her mouth.

Realizing she was being rude, Jill struggled to chew and swallow fast. "I'm sorry. Are you hungry? There's food." She motioned toward the fridge.

"Any eggs and bacon in there?" he asked.

"No, sorry. Fruit? English muffin?" The expression on Aaron's face as he wrinkled his nose in distaste had Jill laughing. "You can order room service if you want."

"Nah, I wouldn't feel right."

It seemed Aaron wasn't interested in CeCe because of her money, or he would be ordering Cristal and caviar and charging it to the room account. Still, CeCe couldn't bring her boy toys home with her, strand them with no ride and not feed them.

"It's not a problem." When he still looked hesitant, Jill added, "I was about to call down and order something for myself."

That appeared to pique his interest. "Really?"

"Yup." Jill nodded. "Want to take a look at the breakfast menu?"

"All right. As long as you were fixin' to order anyway."

Where she currently lived didn't provide much opportunity for hearing colorful language such as *fixin'*.

Smiling at his turn of phrase, she reassured him, "I am." Jill was about to head for the desk where she'd seen a menu when they'd checked in but paused and glanced back. "You might want to put on some clothes though."

He glanced down as if realizing for the first time his lack of clothing. "Jeez. I'm so sorry."

"It's all right." Jill wasn't complaining.

His dark-colored briefs covered him, even if they did hint—quite strongly—at what lay beneath.

The rest of him, all that exposed skin, was smooth and near perfect, save for a few bruises. But having seen him ride and fall last night, the discolorations only added to his appeal in Jill's mind. They were the marks of a champion, and he'd worked hard to get them.

With his lean muscles and hard body, Aaron was nearly underwear-model perfect . . . and Jill was very sure CeCe would not take kindly to finding her hookup in this state of undress with an employee.

He hooked a thumb toward the bedroom door. "I didn't want to wake her before, but I'll just go grab my clothes."

CeCe slept like the dead, so Jill wasn't worried. "I'll get that menu while you do."

"All right." He planted the bottle of water on the counter and turned toward the bedroom, treating Jill to another look at the rear view.

At least there weren't any scratch marks on his back from CeCe's talons. Jill could happily live without seeing that. Knowing her boss had spent the whole night in bed with this incredible cowboy specimen was one thing. Seeing the physical evidence of her passion was another.

She sighed. One day her prince would come. Or billionaire. Or bull rider. Jill wasn't picky. It still seemed unfair that CeCe had already had two out of the three.

Hell, Jill didn't know all that much about CeCe's youth. Maybe there had been a prince in her past and she was three for three. Jill wouldn't put it past CeCe to have scooped a member of a royal family during her modeling career. All that jet-setting through Europe had to make for some interesting encounters with nobility.

Envy. One of the seven deadly sins, the most pointless of all human emotions, and Jill had it bad. She couldn't help it. Especially when Aaron walked back into the room, wearing his jeans this time and carrying his T-shirt.

He reached up, stretched it over his head and pulled it down that perfect torso. Jill stared, unable to do anything else.

"Glad I had a clean T-shirt in my gear bag or else I'd have to wear my riding shirt from yesterday."

Ah, yes. The walk of shame—

"Indeed, being seen wearing the same clothes you left in the night before would be pretty obvious." In Jill's personal experience, it had always been her sneaking in the morning after in last night's heels and makeup, but apparently bull riders had the same fear, just different attire.

Aaron looked amused. "I meant I tried to brush off the dirt, but my shirt took the brunt of my wreck yesterday, and it shows in the amount of dirt ground into the shoulder."

"Oh. That's what you'd meant."

Grinning, he shook his head. "You don't pull any punches, do you, girl?"

"Not if I can help it." She bit her tongue plenty of times in the course of her job, but in real life Jill made it a policy to call it like she saw it. She pushed the menu toward him. "Choose and I'll call it in."

Sitting in the chair opposite Jill, he glanced down at the menu open on the table and then back up at her. "You sure this is okay?"

"I swear. We have an expense account for food when we travel. It's expected."

Even CeCe wasn't such a bitch she wouldn't feed her booty call. She'd want him to be well fueled in case she woke up horny.

After another hesitation, he nodded. "All right. Steak and eggs. Steak, medium rare. Eggs, over easy. White toast. And orange juice, please."

He'd obviously gotten over his reluctance to order anything and was going all in. She could appreciate a man who enjoyed a good hearty breakfast. "Impressive."

He laughed. "Why? What are you getting?"

She'd been considering going healthy. Egg-white omelet maybe, or the yogurt and granola, but after watching Aaron's reckless abandon, Jill ditched that in favor of her original idea. "Eggs Benedict."

He dipped his head. "Impressive, as well."

Jill lifted one shoulder. "I figure that's something I'll never make for myself at home so . . ."

"Then it's an excellent choice." He smiled and her gaze dropped to the dimple in his chin. Jill imagined nibbling on it and had to yank her mind off that image.

Enough of that. She pulled the room phone closer, dialed for room service and placed the order while he watched. Feeling uncomfortable at the attention, Jill hung up and said, "They said half an hour."

"All right. I won't starve in the next thirty minutes—most like." He grinned.

"I hope not. I'd hate to have to explain the body. I mean, I'm the best public relations exec in the company, but still."

He laughed, and she couldn't help focusing on his lips, and then thinking about his lips on CeCe.

Shaking off that thought, she went on, "So you ride again today?"

"Yup. This afternoon. And actually, there's a rider meeting before it, so I'm going to have to get after we eat. I should text Garret. See if he's awake and can come get me." He leaned back and pulled his cell out of his jeans pocket, staring down as he punched in the text.

"If he's not awake, seriously, you can take the limo."

"Let's see about Garret and Chase first. I can't call Skeeter and Riley. They're driving the big stock trailer for this event."

That elicited a burst of a laugh from Jill. "Sorry. It's just I can only imagine what the management of the Mandarin, not to mention the valet, would think about that big stock trailer pulling up to the front door to pick you up."

Aaron let out a snort. "Yeah. You're probably right about that." He raised those violet-blue eyes to her. "So what did I miss last night? And how'd you end up hooking up with a bunch of no good bull riders at a townie bar?"

He sounded wistful. Like he would have rather been out with her and his friends than with CeCe last night.

Interesting.

"Garret found me standing at the door of the arena waiting for a cab."

"Oh, yeah, cabs don't like to come out to that arena. Too far from town."

She nodded. "So I've been told. It would have been nice to know that beforehand."

"You should have taken the limo." He was being a smart ass, trying to pay her back for pushing the limo on him.

Jill cocked a brow. "I would have loved to, but it was otherwise occupied at the time."

And in fact, she should bring some antibacterial wipes with her and wipe down the back seats, because she hated to even think about what might be on them.

"Oh, yeah. I forgot." He had the decency to look contrite, pressing his lips together as his gaze dropped away from hers.

"Anyway, Garret told me he was meeting everybody at the bar for beer and hot wings, so I went along."

"Damn. Hot wings sound good."

"It's morning."

"I know, but I'm really hungry."

She laughed and went on with her story. "So things were pretty quiet until I bought a round of shots . . . and then another."

"Shots." He raised his brows high. "What kind of shots?"

Aaron must suffer from envy too, judging by his level of interest in every detail of last night. The grass was always greener . . . A man can't have limo sex and a night with CeCe Cole and be out with his buddies at the bar at the same time.

"Garret wanted Slippery Nipples but I ordered Fireball. My round, my choice."

Aaron laughed. "Garret's always ordering those. I think he just likes the name of that one. It's kind of too sweet actually."

"Well, I wasn't going up and ordering four Slippery Nipples, that's for damn sure."

He grinned. "Embarrassed?"

"Yes." She nodded.

It was easy talking to him. Too easy. She'd have to remember to keep her distance today at the event. CeCe hadn't looked too happy yesterday when Jill had talked too much to Aaron.

"So after the shots . . ." he prompted her to continue.

"The karaoke girl set up."

"And it was all downhill from there." Aaron smiled wide. "Things got ugly, I bet."

"No. Not so bad. Skeeter and Riley did that old Sonny and Cher song. It was pretty cute. And I still think that Chase, Garret and me doing that Band Perry song kicked some serious musical ass. I'll have to look at the video Skeeter shot on his phone now that I'm sober to be sure though."

Aaron laughed. "Damn. I'm sorry I missed it."

"So am I." More than he could know.

The bedroom door opened and CeCe stood in it, looking less than happy. "Aaron."

He stood and turned. "Hey. Good morning."

"Good morning. What are you doing?" CeCe's gaze cut from Aaron to Jill, the suspicion and curiosity clear in her expression.

Amazingly, she had already applied a full face of make-up, even though Jill was sure she'd love Aaron to believe she woke up looking so put together naturally.

"Waiting on breakfast." Aaron had no idea the minefield he was in the middle of.

Jill scrambled to get them both out of it. "I was making a pot of coffee for you and Aaron came out looking for food, so I told him to order room service."

"Oh." Pasting on a smile, CeCe stepped forward toward Aaron, hooking her arm possessively through his.

Jill stood. There was no excuse or explanation that would ease CeCe's displeasure at having found her boy toy with Jill alone. Time to make an escape and quick. "I'm heading back to my room. I've still got some work to get done this morning."

Aaron turned to frown at her. "Wait. What about your eggs?"

"Um, can you send the guy next door with them when he gets here?"

"All right. I can do that." He nodded.

"Thanks." Jill grabbed her coffee cup.

She was willing to bow out gracefully. Leave CeCe to devour Aaron for breakfast if that's what her boss wanted to do, but Jill would be damned if she was going to sacrifice her morning cup of coffee.

CeCe intently watching the interaction between her and Aaron had Jill forgoing the instinct to say she'd see him later at the event. Instead, Jill took the safer, more conservative course of action. She remained silent and left.

Hopefully, Aaron would soothe CeCe's ruffled feathers.

Jaw clenched as she envisioned the many ways Aaron could do that, Jill retreated to her dark, lonely room.

CHAPTER TWELVE

"You two get settled up here and I'll be back."

"Don't go." CeCe clamped down on Aaron's arm.

He frowned at her hand wrapped around his bicep. "CeCe, I'm coming right back. I've just got to prep my rope."

"Can't someone else do that for you?"

Oh, yeah, that would go over real well. Because his friends wouldn't mock him forever if he told them he couldn't prep his own damn bull rope because last night's hookup wouldn't let him leave her side.

Even Garret, legally part of Aaron's family by marriage, would never let him get away with that shit, and he wouldn't blame him.

"No, I can't ask anybody to do that. They have their own shit to get ready."

She was being ridiculous. Insane. Like stalker crazy.

Oh, Jesus. What if CeCe turned out to be a crazy stalker?

He'd assumed this weekend with him was just a diversion for her. At least, he'd hoped that was it.

Just a divorced woman sowing her wild oats with a younger man now that she was free from her ex-husband. But this behavior, not to mention her death grip on his arm, set off the warning bells in his head. As did the killer look CeCe had shot Jill simply for talking to him this morning.

Not good. In fact, this could turn out to be very bad. Very, very bad. And what the hell could he do about it? Tell Tom Parsons? That wouldn't go over too well either.

Aaron had a suspicion that Tom and the association wouldn't give a crap if it turned out that CeCe was bat-shit crazy. Her money still kept this circuit running.

"CeCe, I swear. I'll be gone ten minutes at the most."

She pouted. At one point yesterday, that no-doubt practiced move had him fantasizing about what her lips could do when wrapped around his cock. Today, he was beginning to realize she used it much too often and the habit made her seem more like a grown woman behaving like a spoiled brat.

"I guess I'm a little oversensitive today. I didn't like waking up in bed alone this morning."

Aaron drew in a breath. "I'm sorry. I told you, I was thirsty and hungry and you were sleeping so soundly I didn't want to wake you."

"Aw, you're so sweet, worrying about me. I'll make sure the front desk knows to bring you anything your little heart desires." She emphasized each word with a tap on his chest.

What his heart desired right now was to prep his damn rope and for her to stop making lovey dovey eyes at him where everyone could see.

He wasn't quite sure if they'd settled things and she was over her possessive fit or whatever this episode was, but he had to get ready. "So I'm gonna prep my rope. All right?"

"Yes, baby. You go. I'll be waiting right here for you."

Great.

"Okay." Aaron knew he needed to make his escape while she was still willing to let him go. Who knew when she'd change her mind.

He spun toward the stairs and came face-to-face with Jill. He'd already learned that CeCe was extra unhappy—and clingy—if he even looked at Jill. He wasn't about to make that mistake now and risk the delicate balance he'd achieved.

"'scuse me." Yanking his gaze away from her, he focused on his boots as he ran down the steps.

Aaron would have to move fast. Dig his glove, rope and rosin out of his gear bag and join his friends where they were already almost done getting ready.

"Jordan." Tom Parson's now familiar voice stopped Aaron in his tracks near the stairs.

He sighed and turned. "Yeah?"

What more could this man assign him to do? He'd already gone above and beyond in his opinion.

"How'd things go yesterday?"

Tom hadn't asked for specifics and Aaron wasn't about to offer. "Things went just fine."

"She's good? You're keeping her happy?"

"Yeah, I'm keeping her happy." As hard as he was working at keeping CeCe Cole happy, and considering some of the things she demanded of him, Aaron should be getting a wad of cash from the association for his efforts.

Hell, what was the going rate for a male escort nowadays anyway?

"You sure she's happy? I don't want her upset. Cole's sponsorship is too important."

Aaron let out a snort, remembering last night. CeCe riding his mouth until she came while his numb hands were tied to her bedposts. After which she'd slid a condom on him and ridden his cock while he was still helpless and bound.

Then this morning, when he'd had to take her to bed before breakfast because she was flustered over waking up alone.

Not to mention how he couldn't even act civil to Jill, just to make sure CeCe didn't get jealous.

"I know that." Oh boy, did he know it. He'd known it when she'd unbuckled his jeans in her limo and also while he'd let her stick her finger in his ass. "And, yes, I am very sure."

"All right. Keep up the good work." Tom turned and disappeared in the direction he'd come from.

Keep up the good work. His job was not done yet. God only knew what else CeCe could possibly do to him that she hadn't already done. Whatever it was, he'd do it. This conversation with Tom Parsons had just ensured that.

"Well, well, well. Look who finally showed up." Garret looked him up and down as Aaron skidded to a stop at his gear bag in the rider room. "Here, I brought you a clean riding shirt."

Pulling open the snaps on his dirty shirt as he shot Garret a glare, Aaron said, "Thanks but you wouldn't have had to bring me a shirt and I wouldn't have missed the meeting if you'd come and gotten me last night when I called. Or this morning when I first texted you."

CeCe had insisted he take the limo to the arena and of course she'd wanted to come with him, making him so late he decided to skip the meeting rather than slide in when it was half over and be embarrassed.

Sure, he'd slept, eaten and showered in a luxurious suite, but the lure of all the many amenities lost something since he'd felt like he was a hostage. Unable to leave when he wanted.

Hell, if he hadn't done exactly what CeCe had wanted this morning after she'd woken up, she probably wouldn't have let him out of the room at all.

Tucking in the clean shirt before he bent to grab his gear out of his bag, Aaron knew he couldn't tell the guys that. Complaining that he had to have sex with a super model this morning before room service arrived in her suite wouldn't get him much sympathy, he was sure.

"Hey, you made your bed, you can lie it in," Garret said as he and Aaron walked out of the rider room.

"What the hell is that supposed to mean?" Aaron glanced at Garret as he looped his rope over the rail. He ran the brush over his rope to knock off any dirt embedded in it.

"It means you chose to take a limo to the hotel of the cougar you rolled around with all night rather than coming out with us. It's not my responsibility to drive you around after. Besides, I never promised to be your ride. If I had promised and then gotten drunk, then you would have something to complain about. We didn't talk about it. You just went off—"

"All right. I get it. It's my own fault for going with her last night." Aaron scowled at the bitter taste of the truth.

"You look awfully unhappy for a man who spent the night getting sweaty with CeCe Cole."

Aaron let out a snort. "CeCe Cole doesn't sweat, believe me."

She was too rich for anything that common. Not to mention she kept the A/C in the bedroom so damn cold it would have been impossible for anyone to perspire.

He'd been freezing the whole night. Maybe she'd wanted it to be so cold in the room so he'd have to spoon her. Whatever the reason, he had gotten a crappy night's sleep.

Aaron yanked one gloved hand down the rope, fast and hard, working the rosin into the fibers. He looked over and found Garret watching him.

"You okay?" There was sincerity in his brother-in-law's question.

His first instinct was to say everything was fine, but the nagging in the back of his brain wouldn't let him deny there was something bothering him.

"I don't know." Aaron glanced up into the stands and saw CeCe watching him. Like a hawk keeping an eye on its prey. He turned away so she couldn't read his lips and kept his voice low as he said to Garret, "I hate to say it, because she's nice and all, but she's acting kind a crazy."

Garret's gaze immediately cut to CeCe and Aaron panicked.

"Don't look!"

Bringing his focus back to Aaron, Garret asked, "Crazy how?"

"She won't let me out of her sight. She insisted on bringing me to the arena. She didn't even want me to leave her long enough to prep my rope."

"Wow." Garret shook his head. "Who would have thought that about her? No offense, but with her money and looks, she could have any guy she wants."

"I know. That's what I thought, but you see it yourself. She's up there watching me. She's waiting for me to get back to her. And she gets upset if I even talk to any other women, including her own employee Jill. I'll be lucky if she lets me leave her to ride."

"Sounds like you got yourself a bunny boiler, kid." At Mustang's mysterious comment, Aaron turned and saw Mustang and Slade standing behind him.

He hadn't noticed that the two riders had wandered over some time during the conversation. He needed to be more careful. He couldn't risk CeCe sneaking up on him.

Mustang's words had Aaron frowning. "I got myself a what?"

"A bunny boiler. You know, like in that old movie. This married guy sleeps with this woman then dumps her. She goes nuts. He and his wife come home and find his kids' pet rabbit boiling in a big pot on the stove."

"You serious?" Garret's eyes widened, while Aaron's blood ran cold.

Mustang snorted. "Hell yeah, I'm serious. Get on your phone and look it up if you don't believe me. *Fatal Attraction* is the name."

"Yup. It's a real movie, all right." Slade dipped his head. "I've seen it. Besides, you really think Mustang could make that kinda shit up?"

Aaron swallowed hard, grateful that any family pets were far away in North Carolina. But, no, that was crazy. CeCe couldn't be that bad. She was just a little . . . needy. He hoped that was it anyway.

"So what are you going to do?" Garret asked.

"I don't know." There was nothing he could do, except hope the remainder of this weekend passed quickly and he could get away clean at the end of it.

Mustang shook his head. "Dump her now, kid, before

things get more serious."

Dump her so she could seek him out later and boil the family cat? Aaron knocked that insane notion out of his head. "I can't dump her."

"Why not?" Slade asked.

"She's a tour sponsor and Tom Parsons assigned him to entertain her. Aaron's on CeCe Cole duty for the duration of the event." Garret answered for him, while Aaron started to fear that she could somehow hear every word.

"*Shh*. You guys gotta all keep your voices down or else she'll hear."

Mustang snorted. "If she planted a bug on you, she's gonna hear no matter how quiet we talk."

"You think she did?" Aaron's gaze whipped to Mustang to find him grinning from ear to ear. "You're fucking with me."

"Me? Never." Mustang feigned shock while next to him Slade snickered.

Talking to these two had only made things worse. Aaron let out a frustrated breath. All he had to do was get through today. He had to try to concentrate enough to ride, and then . . . He had no idea.

He'd have to decide what to do about CeCe. He could suck it up and spend another night with her if he really had to, but damn, he didn't want to.

This was very possibly a first. He had a willing, attractive woman and he wanted nothing to do with her. That right there was concrete proof of how worried he was about this whole situation.

Crap. If he got out of this weekend alive and still on the pro tour roster, he might seriously consider giving up women for good.

Okay, maybe not for good, but at least for a little while. No need to be too drastic.

CHAPTER THIRTEEN

"Are you ready to go?" CeCe wrapped both hands around Aaron's arm like a tourniquet.

He was ready except for the fact he hadn't figured out yet how to get out of it.

"Jordan!" At the sound of his name, Aaron glanced down. He had to stifle a groan at what he saw. Tom Parsons standing with the tour photographer. "Smile."

Aaron was definitely in no mood to smile.

In the presence of the camera, CeCe pulled Aaron closer and smiled wide. Not being a professional model or actor or camera hound, Aaron had to work a little harder. He attempted a smile that felt as forced as he was sure it looked.

Tom was smiling plenty wide though. Apparently, he liked that CeCe had claimed Aaron as her beau for this weekend. He was probably seeing dollar signs.

If Aaron had a brain in his head, he'd be doing the same. CeCe's sponsorship for his career would be nice to have, but he knew it would cost him. She'd own him. No amount of money was worth a piece of his soul.

He'd finish out this weekend because Tom expected it, but that was it. After this three-day event was over and CeCe flew away to wherever she came from, Aaron would have a talk with Tom. Maybe the man didn't realize what CeCe was like. What she expected from him.

Well, Aaron knew now, and Tom couldn't expect Aaron to continue doing what he'd been doing. He wasn't some gigolo, but he was in this now so he'd have to see it through.

Once the posing for more pictures was done, there was no excuse not to go back to CeCe's hotel room. "I'm done. We can go."

She beamed with a smile. "Good."

What was wrong with him? A beautiful woman wanted nothing more than to have sex with him. He should be happy.

Back a few years ago, before veteran riders like Slade and Mustang had gotten girlfriends, they would have given CeCe a run for her money. Hell, if the rumors were true, she could have had them two at a time. Yet all Aaron wanted to do was ditch CeCe and go for a cold one with the guys and Jill.

He stifled a sigh. Time to man the hell up.

"You taking the limo?"

CeCe turned toward the stairs at that question and there stood Jill, looking uncertain. "Oh, I forgot about you. You can find a taxi, can't you?"

Jill's smile looked forced. "Of course. No problem."

Aaron knew it was indeed a problem, but he wasn't about to contradict CeCe. However, a plan began to form in his mind. "I forgot to tell Garret something. You want to wait right here? Or can I meet you out by the limo?"

CeCe looked unhappy to be put off, but she said, "I'll meet you outside. Come, Jill. Walk me out. I want to talk to you about the schedule."

Her taking Jill with her put a kink in his plan, but that was okay. Aaron would just do as he'd said, find Garret and employ his help.

He ran for the rider room and found his brother-in-law inside. Tossing his gear bag on the bench, Aaron dug inside and finally came up with his keys. "Will you do me a favor?"

"No, I can not play stunt cock for your bunny boiler. I'm married to your sister."

"Ha, ha." Aaron held out the keys to his truck. "Will you ask Jill if she'll drive my truck to CeCe's hotel? That way she's not stuck without a ride."

"And you're not stuck with CeCe without a means of escape." Garret cocked a brow while reaching for the keys.

"Yeah, that too." Besides not liking the feeling of being trapped, Aaron had to get some sleep. Getting away from CeCe tonight was the only way he would. The bulls were extra rank on Championship Sunday. He needed his rest to fact them. "Thanks, man."

"No problem. Text me if she ties you to the bed and you need to be rescued."

Aaron choked on his own spit. How the hell did Garret know about that? He hadn't told a soul. "What?"

"You know, like in *Misery*. That Steven King movie where the obsessed chick ties the guy to the bed then breaks both his legs so he can't get away."

"Jesus Christ, you people watch some sick fucking movies." Aaron shook his head, but the whole scenario hit a little too close to home for him.

Garret shrugged. "Just saying."

"Yeah, well, keep it to yourself." Aaron grabbed his bag. "I gotta go. Don't forget about Jill and the keys."

"I won't forget. And Chase and I will keep the cot in our room for you. You know, just in case you manage to escape tonight and need a place to crash."

Aaron turned his back on Garret's cocky grin and trotted to catch up to CeCe before she missed him and had a meltdown. Though now that Garret had mentioned it, his escaping free and clear tonight was a concern.

When had sex become so complicated?

Sadly, that answer was obvious. It was when he'd started having it with the owner of Cole Shock Absorbers.

Aaron pushed through the arena's front door and saw the limo parked along the curb. He tried to look nonchalant as he jogged over, since the same driver as yesterday stood next to the car waiting for him.

As the driver reached out to open the door, Aaron braced himself for anything. For all he knew, CeCe could be stretched out naked on the backseat.

He held his breath until he saw she was sitting, prim and proper and still clothed. He glanced at the driver before tossing his gear bag onto the floor and then sliding inside himself. "Thanks."

The driver nodded his acceptance of the gratitude, but Aaron couldn't shake the feeling that the man was amused by the whole situation. He supposed he couldn't blame him. He and CeCe hadn't exactly been discreet yesterday.

How did he get himself involved in these kinds of embarrassing, not to mention sticky situations?

In future, Aaron would make sure to try his best to avoid them. For now, he had to make it through tonight and tomorrow. Then he and Garret would jump into his truck and head home to North Carolina for a two-week break. He sure as hell could use it.

The driver slammed the door and Aaron was confined alone with CeCe. She moved closer and laid one hand on his chest.

"Hey." CeCe sounded super sexy as she greeted him.

"Hey." To not give her any ideas that he was more interested than he was, Aaron made sure he did not match her tone.

"I'm excited about tonight." She ran one finger up and down his chest. He supposed he should be grateful she hadn't already unbuckled his pants. If she waited until they got to the hotel, today was definitely an improvement over yesterday.

"Yeah?" He really didn't want to ask her why she was excited. He was pretty sure he wouldn't like the answer.

"Mmm, hmm." She didn't elaborate and he didn't prompt her to.

CeCe rested her head on his chest and was quiet, and that

was fine with Aaron. She didn't want to have semi-public sex. She wasn't making him keep up small talk. That might not be the case once they arrived at the hotel, but for now, it was all good.

They did eventually get there. The trip seemed much longer this time since he wasn't occupied as he had been yesterday.

She smiled up at him and squeezed his hand in hers. "We're home, and wait until you see what I have waiting for you."

He was a little scared about what that could be. "What's waiting for me?"

"You'll see."

"I want to know now."

She sighed deeply. "Okay, spoil sport. I had the hotel send up dinner for us. Since you didn't eat at the arena, I figured you'd be hungry."

He hadn't eaten since breakfast. And since she had never taken her damn eyes off him except when he'd gone to the men's room to take a piss, she knew that.

"Oh, okay. Thanks."

"You're welcome. Anything for you, sweetie."

This new attitude of CeCe's had a creepy feel to it. Like she had put herself in the role of happy housewife, with him in the role of husband and the Mandarin was their house. The whole thing was strange.

The driver took forever to open the door, and even then he did it slowly, as if he expected them to be naked. Aaron couldn't say he blamed him. Luckily, this time they were both fully clothed.

Aaron was more than ready to get out of the car and away from the overly observant driver. About as anxious as he was to get away from CeCe and her weird and sudden attachment to him when this weekend was finally over. He had a responsibility to fulfill, and he'd do it, but when it was done, he and Tom Parsons were going to have a little chat.

They walked through the lobby, her hanging on his arm

the entire way. Up in the suite, there were indeed two place settings laid out on the table.

"Go shower. Dinner should be here by the time you get done."

"All right." He certainly didn't mind her kick-ass bathroom with the full body showerheads.

He took an extra long, steamy shower, enjoying the killer water pressure, a luxury he didn't always have at the hotels he stayed in.

By the time he flipped off the water and stepped out of the stall, the room was thick with steam. He reached for a towel to dry off, glanced around the floor for his clothes . . . and found they weren't there.

Frowning, he cracked the door open. "CeCe, did you take my clothes?"

"Yes." She called her answer to him from the other room. "They were all dusty. You don't want to put them back on after you got all clean from your shower. Put on the bathrobe."

His riding clothes were dusty, but he had clean socks, underwear, T-shirt and jeans in his gear bag, which he noticed was also not in the bedroom where he'd left it by the bathroom door.

Being single and living alone for the past few years, he was used to things being where he left them. Even traveling and rooming with a bunch of guys, his stuff might get shoved to the side or get buried under something else, but no one ever outright took it.

Sighing, he reached for the robe and slipped his arms into the sleeves. He had to admit it was thick and fluffy. Pretty damn comfortable actually. Still, he'd rather she leave his shit alone.

After running the towel over his head one more time to get most of the water out of his hair, he tossed it onto the hook and wandered out of the bathroom.

Barefoot, he crossed the bedroom and felt the thickness of the plush carpeting beneath his soles. No doubt about it, there were some major differences between paying under a hundred bucks a night for a hotel room and upwards of five-hundred a night, maybe more considering this was a suite.

And for the pleasure of enjoying it, all he had to do was anything and everything CeCe wanted, right down to wearing a bathrobe to dinner. It seemed eerily similar to that Julia Roberts and Richard Gere movie about the hooker and the millionaire. He pushed the thought out of his mind. That scenario hit a bit too close to home for his taste.

Covered plates were set out on the table and Aaron realized how hungry he actually was. Smiling and looking disturbingly like a housewife, CeCe jumped up from her seat and lifted the covers off the plates. "I hope you like it."

"What is it?"

"Salad made from endive, radicchio, pears and blue cheese. Halibut encrusted with parmesan and a side of roasted cauliflower."

"Oh." He saw her react to his lack of enthusiasm. CeCe's smile disappeared and her mood visibly fell. He scrambled to appease her. "That all sounds really good. Thank you."

He was more of a steak and mashed potato kind of guy. The only thing close to salad that he ate on a regular basis was if his hamburger came with a slice of lettuce and tomato, but that was best kept to himself.

The oddest thing—besides that this was feeling like some sort of married persons' date night—was that she hadn't made a physical move on him yet. It was the opposite of yesterday when she'd started the moment they'd slammed the limo door.

The whole weekend was strange. As if they were on some sort of accelerated timeline. They'd gone from strangers, to sex-starved lovers, to a boring couple all within the span of twenty-four hours.

Good thing he was leaving tomorrow for home, or who knew what would happen next. He could end up picking out china patterns and making seating charts for the wedding if CeCe had her way.

He tightened the belt on the robe to make sure nothing was hanging out that shouldn't be and then sat. He stabbed the fork into the fish and found the flesh flaky and white.

The flavor was amazing and he had to admit, though it wouldn't have been his choice, CeCe had made a good selection. The fish made up for the fancy plate of bitter greens where a plain old lettuce salad would have done just fine.

Dinner passed far too quickly. Partly because he really had been hungry and the food, except for that salad, was good. Partly because it was easier to keep his mouth busy chewing than feel like he had to make small talk with a woman he really didn't know at all but had spent way too much time with the past two days.

But finally, the plates were empty. The bottle of beer she'd ordered him was too. Then there was nothing to do except the obvious. Unless he could come up with an alternate plan . . .

He glanced at the huge television and got an idea. "Anything good on the movie channels?"

"Maybe." CeCe's voice dipped low as her eyes narrowed. She stood and swayed her way around to him. Squeezing herself in the narrow space between him and the table, she straddled him in his chair. "We can check that out on the television in the bedroom."

He hadn't been talking about *those* kinds of movies, but as she wiggled in his lap and pressed her tits into his face, he got the feeling she was.

"I'm going to go get ready. You wait here until I call you."

"Okay." What else could he say?

Looking incredibly excited for whatever she had planned, CeCe scampered off to the bedroom.

A couple of minutes later, she said, "I'm ready. You can come in."

A little afraid of what he'd find, Aaron pushed the door to the bedroom open.

CeCe sat naked in the center of the bed. She crooked a

finger at him. "Drop the robe and come here."

Seeing no way out, he did. Crawling naked onto the bed, he was hoping for a round of normal sex. He'd even snuggle afterward if it made her happy and meant she'd just go to sleep.

When she pulled a long black strap from beneath the pillow, he knew his hope was in vain. "What's that?"

"A harness."

Panicked, he shook his head. "I don't want my hands tied again."

That damn movie about the chick who broke the guy's legs so he couldn't get away flashed through Aaron's mind. He silently cursed Garret for putting it in his head.

"This isn't for your hands." She looped the padded strap around the back of his neck and then brought the two ends forward in front of him. "Lie back."

"What are you—"

"You are full of questions today." She gave him a little shove and he landed on his back. "Knees bent."

"What?"

"Bring your knees up to your chest."

He did it even while saying, "CeCe, I'm not sure about this."

She fastened each end of the strap around his thigh and buckled it. He realized it kept his legs up and wide open, giving her total access to every part of him.

"The straps are a little short," he said, more than uncomfortable.

"Just the way they're supposed to be." She smiled as she patted his bare buttocks with her open palm.

He talked himself down from the panic overtaking him. His hands were free. If he had to, he could get out of the restraints. He wasn't completely at her mercy.

She leaned over to the bedside drawer and emerged with a tube of lubricant. Aaron's pulse pounded in his ears as she moved to between his legs.

Her finger, slick and cool, breached him, pushing past

muscles hell bent on keeping her out. "You know I used to do this to Mr. Cole."

Now she wanted to talk? While she was lubing up his ass? "No. I didn't know."

"He'd get on his hands and knees and he'd beg me for it. Asked me to fuck him in his ass, tell me to use the biggest dildo I had in my strap-on."

Oh my God. Was that what she wanted from him? Had last night been just the warm up?

"I—" He had to swallow to get the rest out. "I wouldn't like that."

"You're nothing like him. You're not a ball-less man who has to prove his masculinity by screwing around with other women." She had him trussed and lubed as she ranted about her ex-husband, and all Aaron could do was hope he wasn't about to be the next recipient of her strap-on.

She leaned for the drawer again and he got scared. "CeCe, what are you doing?"

"You'll see."

That was the problem. He couldn't see. "Please tell me."

"I'm going to make you feel good."

His breath was coming fast. In fact, it wouldn't surprise him one bit if he hyperventilated.

"You don't have a strap-on in there, do you?" He joked, but his fear was very real. He had jumped on the back of the rankest bulls in the circuit with less fear-fueled adrenaline than he felt now.

"Not yet." Her words sent a panic through him.

"CeCe, please."

"That's what I like to hear. You begging for it." She was back between his legs again and even as cold as the room was, Aaron began to sweat.

He heard the buzz before he felt it pressing against his hole. He jumped. "What is that?"

"It's just a teeny tiny treat for you. Relax."

That elicited a nervous laugh from him. Relax? In this position? Was she crazy?

"I promise. You're going to love it."

That was the other problem. Not his biggest concern at the moment, but definitely one of them. He didn't want to like it.

"So do you, like, travel with this stuff?" he asked, both curious and hoping to distract her as she held the vibrator against him.

"Oh, no. I had it all delivered to the hotel today."

He lifted his head to see her bent between his legs, concentrating hard. "You had it delivered?"

"Mmm, hmm."

He opened his mouth to ask from where, but his words didn't come out because at that moment she'd pushed the toy in. He clenched and hissed in a breath.

"I said relax."

"That's easy to say." Aaron was the one in restraints, not her.

"And easy to do. What's the matter? You were fine yesterday."

"Yesterday was your finger. Not a—whatever that is. And yesterday, you were blowing me at the same time."

"It's a thin vibrator. And I really detest that term you just used for what's a beautiful act." Her brow creased.

She pushed the vibe deeper and he stiffened even as he felt the need to apologize for offending her. "Sorry."

"Not a problem. Now you know my feelings on the matter. And your hands aren't tied, feel free to distract yourself."

She wanted him to play with himself now too? In front of her. Because it wasn't humiliating enough she was sliding something long and hard inside him.

"Aaron, sweetheart. Trust me."

He feared he'd regret it later, but he drew in a breath and said, "Okay."

"Good. Close your eyes."

"Why? What are you going to do?" He lifted his head again, concerned.

"Nothing. I want you to concentrate on what you're feeling and you won't if you keep trying to see."

"Oh. All right." Breathing out, long and slow, Aaron did as she asked. He pressed his head back against the pillow and closed his eyes.

He'd willingly put himself in this position. He'd committed to seeing tonight through. Of course, that was before the word strap-on had been mentioned. But so far, thankfully, one hadn't appeared.

If the vibe kept her happy, he'd deal with it. He'd be glad when it was over, but he'd power through.

Reaching down, he felt for his cock, slack in his grasp. He let himself concentrate on the sensations ripping through him, the vibrations that were as disturbing as they were pleasant.

CeCe moved the vibe, pulling it out and then pushing it back in, just a bit. She repeated the process and his cock started to harden in his grasp. He felt her move. A stream of cold hit him. He opened his eyes and watched CeCe drizzle lube over his fist and growing erection.

He leaned back and closed his eyes again. Hell, if he was going to do this, and do it in front of her, while she did that, he might as well go all out. He tugged in earnest now, figuring the sooner he came, the faster it would all be over. She'd have to stop then.

She zeroed in on one spot, pressing the toy against an area inside him that had his body jerking like he'd been electrocuted.

The vibrations went from making him have to gasp for breath, to hard enough he let out a shout. CeCe must have hit the next speed on the toy.

He would have jerked away from the overwhelming sensation if he weren't in his current position. With his legs held up and wide, all CeCe had to do was follow him the couple of inches he moved when he tried to yank away from her.

"Just let go and enjoy it." She pressed the vibe against that spot again and Aaron had no choice but to do as she suggested.

He felt the orgasm start deep inside him even before the physical evidence shot into the air. He had no control of his body as the sensations burned a path through him like lightning.

Noises he was sure he'd never made during sex before filled the bedroom, no doubt penetrating the walls into the other room. Then again, this wasn't sex.

This was some sort of battery-operated torture this woman had devised to keep him at her mercy. Torture was the only word he could come up with for uncontrolled pleasure that bordered on pain and filled him with humiliation and shame.

Even so, there was the undeniable fact that this kinky shit did it for him. He wouldn't have come so hard if it didn't.

She kept the toy inside him. Even after he'd run dry, he felt his muscles still rhythmically contracting around the hard plastic invading him.

"No more. I can't take anymore." He gasped the plea.

She turned the vibrations to low, but in his over-sensitized state, that was still too much. He tried to pull away from her and she finally switched the toy off.

"Mmm. That was nice." She didn't take the damn thing out of him. She continued to move it, ever so slowly. Even if it was off now, she continued to work him with slow movements that made his body jerk every time she hit that one spot.

"Um, CeCe? Can you take that out now?"

"Get hard again for me, lover. You're young. You can do it. I know you can."

Young or not, Aaron had no clue how he was going to get hard anytime soon. He was weak. His arms felt like lead. He didn't even have enough energy left to move his hands. Never mind enough to stroke himself into another erection, even if he wanted to.

But if nothing else, he knew one thing. What CeCe

wanted, CeCe got. Tonight, she wanted him.

"CeCe, I need some time."

"I know what's wrong. You're too used to this toy now. You need something bigger." She pulled out the vibrator but Aaron felt no relief as she moved toward the nightstand.

Bigger. His heart began to pound like a jackhammer at the thought.

His cock jerked beneath his hand as he started to grow hard. His ass clenched as she reached for the drawer and he anticipated what she'd do to him next.

He could never ever breathe a word of this to any of the guys.

Yes, they'd understand his keeping a sponsor happy for the good of the association. And get that he enjoyed getting naked after an event with a hot-as-hell, not to mention rich older woman. That was totally understandable. Any number of riders would be envious of him and the time he got to spend in the lap of luxury with her.

But the fact he was now hard as a rock from watching her lube up a vibrator twice the size of the last one so she could stick it inside him—the guys would never understand that.

Hell, Aaron didn't understand it himself, but as she moved toward him again, he couldn't think about anything but how the hell that thing was going to fit inside him.

CeCe smiled and flipped on the vibrator. "I think you're going to like this one."

As she pressed it against him, Aaron closed his eyes and blocked out the knowledge that this one was far too phallic-looking for his taste. That was right before she eased it deep inside him and he started not to care anymore.

CHAPTER FOURTEEN

"So how's your trip?" The excitement in Jackie's voice was evident. Jill's sister and best friend could make anything sound exciting, even a business trip.

"It's fine." Aside from the fact she'd had to watch, and then hear, her boss hooking up with a hot young bull rider.

Jill kept that part to herself. But damn, the sounds coming out of CeCe's bedroom, which Jill heard from two rooms away, were enough to fuel a girl's curiosity as much as her disgust about what was happening in there.

Added to Jill's sexual frustration was the fact that Jackie was much too perky and awake. It might be evening in California where Jill lived, but here on the East Coast it was time for her to be in bed. But just because the clock said Jill should be sleeping, didn't mean her body agreed.

"Is it a nice city?" her sister asked, ever curious.

Jill let out a snort of a laugh. First of all, she wasn't sure Duluth, Georgia, where the event was being held, was all that known for its tourist attractions. Aside from that, she'd never been on a business trip where she'd gotten to see anything.

"I really wouldn't know. I've seen the airport, the hotel and the arena. Oh, and one local bar where I had drinks with some of the riders."

"Ooo. That last part sounds interesting. Do tell."

Jackie always was an optimist, looking for a love connection for Jill even when there was none. "Don't get excited, sis. Every one of them was taken."

"Every single one? Aren't there any single bull riders?"

"There are a few riders who are single, but they weren't with us last night."

And one of those single bull riders was now taken, if the way CeCe had been hanging all over Aaron at the event was any indication.

It was the story of Jill's life. Always the bridesmaid and never the bride. Hell, she didn't even need the whole diamond ring and white dress. Just a night or two of hot sex would do. One weekend of the kind of red-hot sex with Aaron that she'd heard through the walls would no doubt hold Jill for months.

Instead, CeCe had gotten that hot weekend and Jill had gotten to work late in her hotel room.

"One day your prince will come. I promise. Mine did."

Yes, her sister's prince had come along years ago in high school, which didn't help Jill's feelings about her single status any.

Jill sighed. "I know."

A knock on the connecting door to the suite had Jill frowning. What the hell did CeCe want with her at this time of night? Especially on a night when she had Aaron in her bed? "Jackie, I gotta get going. I'll call you tomorrow."

"All right. Night."

"Goodnight." Jill ended the call and tossed her phone onto the bed.

She reached for the knob and pulled open the door. There stood Aaron, his boots held in one hand and his bag in the other.

"Can I come in?" He spoke like a man in hiding, his voice soft and anxious.

"Um, yeah. Sure." Jill took a step back to let him in. CeCe

would flip if she saw Aaron here, but Jill was too curious to tell him no.

He glanced over his shoulder one more time before following her in and pulling the door closed behind him. "I'm sorry to bother you so late."

"Not a problem. I was awake." And now she was incredibly interested to know why Aaron was sneaking out of CeCe's suite like a thief in the night.

"Do you have my keys?"

His purpose for being in her room became clear. His truck keys. He was indeed making an escape, and Jill would bet her paycheck that CeCe was asleep and knew nothing about his quiet departure.

"Keys?" Jill used every ounce of acting ability she had to play dumb. She sounded pretty convincing, if she did say so herself.

His eyes widened as his mouth dropped open. "You didn't drive my truck here?"

Aaron's expression was so priceless, it was all Jill could do to maintain her composure and not laugh. Actually, she couldn't for very long.

She ended up smiling and letting him off the hook. "Just kidding. Yes, I have your truck. Garret gave the keys to me."

"Oh, thank God." He let out a breath so filled with obvious relief it made Jill wonder even more about what could have happened.

She'd been about to thank him for providing her with a means of transportation after CeCe had told her to call a cab, but as Jill moved to retrieve the keys, she had to think that she'd done him the favor, not the other way around.

Jill grabbed her bag where she'd stashed Aaron's keys. She had figured she'd be driving Aaron's monster truck back to the arena in the morning. Of course, that was back when she'd thought he'd be riding with CeCe in the limo again. Back before she'd been aware of his midnight plan to flee.

He took a step forward, but she wasn't about to let him off that easily.

"Oh, no. Not so fast." Keys still held captive in her hand, she pulled them away from his reaching grasp. "You don't get these until you tell me why you're sneaking out."

And looking so desperate to do it without CeCe knowing.

"No reason." Aaron was a horrible liar. She heard the underlying panic in his voice.

Now she was really curious. Jill crossed her arms and waited.

He must have finally realized he wasn't getting his keys without some sort of explanation. Aaron let out a sigh. He put his bag down on the floor and sat in her desk chair.

"I just need to get a good night's sleep before tomorrow's event." Avoiding eye contact, Aaron focused on his feet as he pulled one boot over his sock.

Him needing a good night's rest before the competition was a valid excuse. She couldn't really argue with him even if she felt deep down there must be more to Aaron's leaving so stealthily. After he'd pulled on the second boot, she held his keys out to him.

He stood and took them. "Thank you."

"You're welcome. Anytime. It's not often I get to drive a big-boy truck like yours. I live in Los Angelis now, so I've got a compact car that's good on gas and is easy to park but my suitcases barely fit."

He smiled, but she could see the weariness in him. "I'd better go."

"Mmm, hmm. You need your rest for tomorrow." She moved to the door—the one that led to the hallway and Aaron's path of escape, not the other door to the suite. "So I'll see you at the arena."

"Yup. You will. Goodnight." He tipped his hat and headed into the hallway, bag in hand.

Jill watched him until he turned the corner for the elevator, wondering if he had always walked as if he was in pain and she just hadn't noticed before, or if he had a new injury from that night's event.

And yes, she also watched because there was something

about a cowboy in jeans and boots that drew a girl's eye. Especially the eye of a displaced country girl now living in a city.

She'd have to visit her family in Virginia and soon.

Possibly look up one of her old boyfriends while she was there. If one was around and still single, she could meet him for a drink . . . and more.

Maybe that would get rid of this ache she got inside her whenever she looked at or thought about Aaron.

Then again, she doubted a substitute would do.

CHAPTER FIFTEEN

"So you're still not going to tell me why Chase and I woke up in the middle of the night to you stumbling around in the dark in our hotel room?"

Wishing everyone would just leave him alone Aaron shook his head and concentrated on pawing through his gear bag in search of his mouth guard.

"Why are you not talking?" Arms crossed, Garret leaned against the wall of the riders' dressing room.

"Garret, just quit. There's nothing to talk about." Aaron finally checked the pocket of his safety vest and found the mouth guard there, right where he'd stashed it after yesterday's ride. Damn, his mind was definitely not on his riding today.

"Really?" The skepticism was clear in his brother-in-law's voice. "You don't want to talk about why, when a gorgeous rich woman invites you to spend the night in her luxury suite, you sneak out to sleep on the cot in our cheap hotel room?"

"I told you already. I needed to get some sleep."

"And you couldn't sleep in her room because why? Does she keep you *up* all night?" Garret waggled his eyebrows as he stressed the word.

Thinking his friend was being more juvenile than clever,

Aaron let out a sound of frustration. "Can we please talk about something else?"

"Sure. How about this for a topic? Is there a reason you're hiding in the rider room instead of hanging with the other guys behind the chutes?"

Aaron was trying to think of a plausible reason, aside from the truth, when Tom Parsons popped his head in the doorway. "Jordan, why the hell are you back here instead of up in the VIP section with CeCe Cole?"

Shit. She was here? Aaron was kind of hoping she wouldn't show. He knew her not coming would be a long shot, but it didn't hurt to wish for it anyway.

Garret looked between Tom Parsons standing in the doorway and to where Aaron slumped on the bench. Both men were waiting for the answer Aaron didn't want to give.

"Um, I'm getting ready."

The head of the association scowled. "Well, hurry the hell up and get out there."

"Yes, sir."

Tom Parsons left, but Aaron still had Garret to deal with . . . and then CeCe after that. Christ. He missed the good old days when the biggest thing he had to deal with at these events was the ton of bovine intent on throwing him into the dirt.

Garret crossed his arms, leveled his gaze on Aaron and waited.

"Fine, I'll tell you." Aaron let out a huff. "I can't take it. Okay?"

"Can't take what?" Garret spread his hands before him, as if lost for an explanation. "The limo? The fancy hotel? The unlimited sex with a hot-as-hell woman?"

"There's other stuff going on." Aaron couldn't bring himself to meet his friend's gaze.

Garret glanced at the open doorway before he moved to the door and shut it. Coming back to Aaron, he straddled the bench and leaned forward. "Talk."

Stuff was an understatement for some of the shit CeCe had

pulled on him last night, the exact details of which he'd never admit to another living soul. But it wasn't the kinky stuff that scared him. It was how quick she was to act like she owned him. "She's too . . . intense."

"You mean like bunny-boiler intense?"

Aaron finally glanced up at Garret. "You're going to use that new term Mustang taught you any chance you get, aren't you?"

"Yup." A grin brightened Garret's face.

"Okay, then, yeah. Intense like that."

"Well, considering you don't have kids or pet rabbits, I think you're safe. She has a huge company to run and a life somewhere far from North Carolina. We've got a couple of weeks off, so she can't even come to any events to find you. She'll have moved on to someone new by then. It's all good." Garret shrugged, as if there was nothing to worry about.

"I guess." Aaron could only hope Garret was right. That he just had to get through today and then everything would be okay. But getting through today might be an issue. "She might be pissed at me now though."

"Why? What did you do?"

"I'm pretty sure she assumed I'd stay the night, but I snuck out while she was sleeping." Aaron cringed.

Saying it out loud made him realize how bad what he'd done was.

Garret lifted his brows high. "You didn't tell her that you had Jill drive your truck there so you could leave?"

"Nope."

"Man." Garret shook his head. "She's gonna be pissed at you, all right. What the hell were you thinking, sneaking out like that? You really don't know women at all, do you?"

Aaron scowled at the insult. "And you do?"

"Yeah. I do."

"How you figure?"

"I'm married to your sister, who's not exactly a pushover, in case you've forgotten. Since I've managed to stay happily married to her, I'm pretty sure I know more about handling

That image was a bit too much of a reminder of the activities of last night. It sent a tremor through him that only grew stronger when CeCe ran one long polished fingernail down his arm.

"In that case, I guess I understand. You should have told me you were leaving."

"You were sleeping so peacefully, I didn't want to wake you up."

"Leaving a note would have been nice."

He hung his head. "You're right. I should have. I apologize."

"All right. I'll forgive you. Of course, you know I won't be able to let such a transgression pass without any consequences. You'll have to be punished." She said it with the sultry voice of a sex goddess, yet her words sent a cold chill of fear down his spine.

"Excuse me?"

"Don't worry, lover. I'm sure you'll enjoy the penance I'll come up with for you tonight."

He had to tell her there would be no tonight. And there sure as hell would be no punishment. He was certain he wouldn't enjoy what she had in mind for him no matter what she said.

"Um, we're heading out tonight. Garret and I are driving home right after the short go." His truck was already packed with their stuff. They'd checked out of the hotel. There was no doubt in his mind. He was not spending tonight with CeCe.

"Who's Garret?"

"My brother-in-law. He and my sister live in the same town that I do. I drove him here in my truck."

"That's perfect. He can drive your truck home while you come with me."

"With you? Nah, I can't do th—"

"It's my understanding there's no competition next weekend." She cut his protest off before she asked, "Correct?"

"No, there's not, but—"

"Then it's settled. You'll fly home with me in the jet." She leaned close and pressed her mouth near his ear. "It's a nice long flight to California. I'll have all night to initiate you into the mile-high club. I can pick up a new toy for you at the store before we leave."

That was not a good plan. So far, CeCe's playthings had progressively gotten bigger and scarier. He didn't even want to imagine what this new selection would be. There'd be no sneaking out on CeCe or escaping her new toy while thirty-thousand feet in the air on her private jet.

As his blood ran cold, the lights dimmed and the music began pumping out of the sound system. "Shit. I gotta get down there for the opening."

Looking like the devil who wanted to own his soul, she smiled. "Hurry back."

"All right." He agreed to that demand, but the rest was an entirely different story.

For now, he had to get his head in the game. There was a rank bull on the roster for the second section with his name next to it. Sad to say, he was way more worried about facing CeCe tonight than that bull.

"Hey." Chase came to stand next to Aaron as they all lined up for the rider introduction.

After that would be the prayer and the singing of the National Anthem. Then he'd have to go back to CeCe instead of doing what he should, focusing on his ride.

Chase leaned in a bit. "Did you see? They swapped some of the bulls around. You're up in the first section now instead of the second."

Aaron's attention whipped to Chase. "No. I didn't see."

His friend nodded. "Yup. You're riding in the first five."

"Thanks for telling me."

He couldn't go anywhere after the opening. He had to be ready to ride or risk a penalty. Even CeCe couldn't argue with that. It was a totally legit reason.

Of course, CeCe didn't always seem to respond to the

logical or the rational. Besides, he'd still have to deal with her after his ride . . . and then after the event.

Crap.

Damn, Tom Parsons.

CHAPTER SIXTEEN

"Next up, Aaron Jordan in the Cole Shock Absorbers chute aboard Willy Wonka. Jordan's teetering on the edge of the top ten in the rankings this event. He needs to make this ride."

"You're right, JW. Jordan could sure use those bonus points from today's short go."

"Of course, Jim, he'll have to ride Willy Wonka to get to the championship round, and this bull is two and ten in this series."

"No doubt about it, JW, this is one rank bull. We've come to expect some good buckers from the Davis pens, and this one doesn't disappoint."

Aaron listened to the announcer's chatter as he wrapped the end of the bull rope around his gloved hand.

The bull stood calmly beneath him, but Aaron wasn't deceived. The minute the gate opened, he'd kick into action.

He knew this animal. He'd seen him buck off ten of his friends.

Hell, he'd fed and watered this damn bull when he and Garret had been helping Riley Davis at her place after her father's death.

None of that was going to do him any good now. The

announcers were correct. Butch Davis had raised good bulls, and Riley hadn't let the business slip even a little after his death.

Once that gate opened, Willy Wonka's sole goal was going to be knocking Aaron off his back. Just as Aaron's only objective was to hang on, at least for eight seconds.

It didn't even have to be pretty. He didn't need a ninety-point ride to qualify for the short go, but he did need a qualified ride and whatever points came with it, no matter how shitty his score.

Aaron pounded his gloved fingers closed around the rope. Flipping the legs of his chaps out of the way with his free hand, he moved his feet back and forth, checking if his spurs were clear of the rope. His mouth guard was in. He was as ready as he was going to get.

"Let's see if Jordan is sticky enough to join the elite club of only two riders to make it to the whistle aboard this bull. And there's the nod."

Aaron stopped paying attention to the announcers' banter as he nodded to the gateman. With one yank of the attached rope, the metal gate swung wide. It landed with a crash against the rails.

At that cue, the bull burst out of the chute and turned into a spin against Aaron's riding hand.

Each powerful leap into the air followed by the crashing of almost a ton of bull back down to the ground jarred Aaron to the bone.

He felt himself slipping, losing his seat. He could have jumped off safely on the outside of the spin, but if he held on for just a few seconds longer, he could make this ride.

It wouldn't be pretty, but if the rope remained in his hand and no part of his body touched the ground, it would count.

He was hanging way off one side of the bull on the inside of the spin, squeezing tight with his legs in a desperate attempt to not hit the dirt before the buzzer.

The animal snapped, changing direction. The quick action sent Aaron flying. He saw the ground rushing toward his face.

He landed hard with the wind knocked out of him.

Riley's bulls were professional athletes. The animal had no interest in Aaron once he was on the ground, which was a good thing, because Aaron needed a few moments to get his wind back.

His wrist hurt where he'd landed on it. His knee felt like it was on fire where it had slammed into the ground. God only knew what else would start to hurt once the adrenaline fled. Then the soreness would begin to creep in. Tomorrow morning, he'd be stiff and achy.

The worst part was he'd heard the eight-second buzzer sound from where he lay in the dirt. There was no chance he'd made the ride and chances were he wouldn't qualify for the top ten riders who got to be in the short go.

Wade Long wandered over. From his position on the ground, Aaron got a good look at the bull fighter's sneakers before the man squatted down and knocked his cowboy hat back. "You a'ight?"

"Yeah. Fine."

"You sure? Nothing broken?"

"I'm sure. Just the wind knocked out of me."

"Good." Wade nodded. "So you planning on getting up any time soon or should I call for some tea and crumpets to be delivered to you right here?"

"Ha, ha. I'm getting up." Aaron let out a sigh and sat up. "Frigging bull. I bet Butch Davis is looking down from heaven and laughing right about now."

"Probably. But that bull did you a favor reversing and launching you off like that, rather than dumping you inside the spin. Another good thing—your spectacular dismount will be one hell of a highlight on YouTube." The man grinned as he extended a hand and hoisted Aaron to his feet.

"Yeah, thanks." Aaron knew everything the man said was true.

The way things were going before the reversal, he would have been under the bull getting trampled. And yeah, a buck-off this showy would be all over the television station's highlight reel and the web. Nothing he could do about it.

"Anytime. Here. Don't forget your rope." Wade thrust his bull rope at him.

"Thanks." Aaron took it and then limped to the out gate.

"That was one hell of a match-up, kid." Mustang grinned from where he stood watching the action.

"Yeah, thanks." Aaron glanced past Mustang and got a look at the VIP section. His head had been so completely on the ride, he'd forgotten about CeCe for a moment. He remembered now though. "Ah, shit."

"What?" Mustang asked.

"I'd forgotten about her."

Mustang turned to glance at CeCe before Aaron could warn him not to. "Your . . . um, *girl?*" He stressed the last word, probably because it was more than obvious CeCe had passed the age where she could be called a girl a few decades ago.

She caught his eye and leaned over the rail. "Are you done riding now?"

"Yeah." Christ. Wasn't it bad enough he'd bucked off so badly he fully expected it to be featured all over the damn place as the wreck of the night? Now he had to deal with her crazy stalker ass too?

Mustang watched the situation with interest.

Aaron sighed. "I can't get away from her. She wants me next to her all the time and now she wants me to go home with her to California."

"Well, you took a hell of a fall out there. I'd think something like that would warrant a visit to sports medicine. And you know, if you maybe had a real painful groin pull from that wreck, that would put you out of commission for a good long time."

Aaron frowned. "I didn't pull my groin. I hit my knee."

Mustang raised a brow, waiting. It took a second, but Aaron's scrambled brain finally caught on. "Oh. You mean fake the injury?"

"Now you're thinking. Sometimes in these situations, a lie

can be the kindest thing. You don't want to hurt her feelings and tell her you're not interested, but you don't want to be with her anymore either, am I right?"

"It's just that she and I have nothing in common. She's way too clingy. She wants to be serious and I don't. And if this goes on any longer, she's going to get more attached and then get hurt when I end it." Guilt made Aaron feel the need to explain.

"I was looking for a simple yes or no, not a song and dance. Do you want to be with this woman or not?" Mustang cocked a brow.

Like it or not, the answer was clear in Aaron's mind. "No."

"Then I say you limp on over there and tell her you need to see the doc. Then don't come back out. Security won't let her into the medical room, even with that VIP pass she's wearing." Mustang was right . . . and brilliant in Aaron's opinion.

"Mustang, you might have saved my ass." Little did his fellow rider know that Aaron meant that literally.

CHAPTER SEVENTEEN

As much as Jill loved watching the bulls and the riders, she was more than happy this event was over.

It was exciting as hell being here live and up close for the rides. But she didn't love being here live for the wrecks, especially since Aaron had been one of the worst buck offs of the day.

Although it was another aspect of this particular three-day long Georgia event that had her feeling more uncomfortable than even watching Aaron launch off the back of his bull. That was having a front row seat, day and night, for CeCe and Aaron's whirlwind romance.

That Jill hadn't bargained on.

It sure as hell wasn't part of her job description, and yet the whole weekend she'd been dancing around this relationship, if she could call it that.

CeCe having sex with Aaron in the suite didn't exactly constitute a love story, but the scene before Jill now sure looked like a lover's spat.

All she'd wanted to do was find CeCe and tell her the pilot was waiting for them at the airport. What she'd found was CeCe and Aaron at the end of a long hallway. She couldn't make out any words, but it was clear from their body language alone that Aaron and CeCe were in the midst of a heated discussion.

Both of their voices got louder until Jill began to be able to make out words. She should have backed away and given them their privacy. She didn't. Instead, curiosity won out. She stayed and listened.

"CeCe, no. I'm not flying home with you. I'm not your boyfriend. We're not dating. It was just a weekend and now it's over."

Jill cringed at Aaron's words. Even if she wasn't the one getting dumped, it was harsh hearing it. She might not be the biggest fan of CeCe Cole, but Jill had been on the receiving end of a dumping more than once. She wouldn't wish what Aaron had said to CeCe on any woman.

She held her breath, waiting for CeCe's response. She expected her to cry and play on his sympathies, but he didn't give her a chance. He turned on one boot heel and, before Jill could react or hide, he was heading down the hallway directly at her.

Jill saw the stiff set of his jaw. The hard, flat expression in his eyes. He met her gaze but didn't say a word as he walked past and around the corner.

She watched him pass and turned back to find CeCe glaring at her. "I'm sure you enjoyed watching that, didn't you?"

"What? No. I mean I couldn't even hear—"

"You've had your eye on Aaron since we met him. You've been jealous of me from day one. I should have known when I woke up that first morning and found you in the suite flaunting yourself in front of him. Cozying up to my boyfriend."

"I never did—"

"Don't bother coming to work in the morning. You're fired." CeCe turned and strode in the opposite direction Aaron had gone while Jill stood in shock.

She was supposed to be on that private flight back to California with CeCe. Now what? Her luggage was already in the limo waiting outside for them. Jill wouldn't put it past CeCe to drive away with it—either intentionally or accidentally.

If that happened, Jill would be stranded with nothing but the tote bag on her shoulder. That thought had Jill running toward the exit. She emerged from the building in time to see the driver slamming the trunk. Her carry-on and suitcase sat on the sidewalk.

The limo driver sent her a sympathetic glance before he slid behind the steering wheel and slammed the door.

Helpless and reeling, Jill stood on the steps and watched her ride pull away. She was stuck, again, at the arena where she already knew taxis didn't like to come to.

Not that it mattered all that much if she couldn't get to the airport any time soon. She had no plane ticket.

With a sigh, she walked the rest of the way down the staircase.

Sitting on top of the suitcase, she made a plan. First on the agenda was to let herself have a good cry, because this had to be the worst day of her life. After that, she'd figure something out.

"Jill!"

The sound of her name brought her head around. Aaron and Garret were walking toward her from around the side of the building.

She swiped the moisture from her eyes as they got close enough to see her sitting on her suitcase crying. She forced a laugh. "I think there's a country song about this very thing."

"Yup, there sure is." Garret nodded.

"What happened?" Aaron frowned and glanced at the parking lot. "Where's CeCe? And where's the limo?"

"Well, the answer to all those questions is pretty much the same. CeCe fired me and left."

"What?" Aaron's eyes went wide. "Why?"

Jill shrugged. "Because she thought I was after you."

His eyes got even wider. "Me?"

She nodded. "Yup. Apparently, I've been flaunting myself

in front of you. So she and her limo and her private jet are heading back to California without me."

"And she left you stranded in Georgia with no transportation?" Garret joined Aaron in his expression of shock.

"Yup. I guess I should be happy that she left me my luggage."

"That is seriously fucked up." Garret shook his head. He glanced at Aaron. "Man, you sure can pick 'em."

"You know damn well I didn't pick her. She was assigned to me." Aaron drew in a breath and looked to Jill. "You're coming with us."

"Where?"

He reached for her carry-on. "Wherever you want us to take you. Get up. Garret, grab the suitcase."

She had to scramble to her feet as Garret moved toward the suitcase she was sitting on.

"Where you wanna go? The airport?" Aaron asked.

Jill stood helpless as the two men took possession of her bags. "I don't know. A last-minute flight to California is going to cost a fortune."

She needed to watch her pennies since she no longer had a job. Jill didn't want to dump over a thousand dollars on a flight that would normally cost a fraction of that if she'd had the liberty of booking in advance.

"Then you're coming home with us." Aaron said it with finality.

"And do what?"

"You book a flight for a later date—whenever you can get a good price—I'll drive you to the airport. Either Charlotte or Raleigh-Durham. You should be able to get a good flight from one of those. In the meantime, you hang with us until you leave."

"I can't do that." Jill had to jog after the two cowboys as they strode across the parking lot. Their long legs ate up the distance even with her luggage slowing them down.

"Sure you can. I have a spare bedroom at my place."

Aaron stopped at the tailgate of his truck and hoisted her carry-on inside. "Besides, it's my fault you got fired. Let me do something to help so I feel less guilty about it."

"Aaron, it's not your fault."

"Sure it is." Garret laughed. "He's the one who couldn't handle your boss."

"Shut up, Garret."

Ignoring their bickering, Jill had to think that it might not be a bad plan. Why should she rush to get back to California? She had no job there. Just a tiny overpriced apartment, which she wouldn't need anymore if she didn't find work in that area.

Aaron opened the truck door. "Hop on in."

She hoisted herself into the high truck. Garret and Aaron got in on either side of her so she was sandwiched between them in the center of the front bench seat.

"My family lives in Virginia. Maybe I should go there and regroup until I decide what to do next. Hell, I don't know." She sighed.

"Maybe." Aaron glanced at her as he turned the key in the ignition. "The point is you don't have to decide this second. Come home with me. Take some time to think. I've got two weeks off from competition. If you want me to, I'll be happy to drive you to your parents' place or wherever you want. It's the least I can do."

Jill shook her head. "Stop saying that. This isn't your fault."

Garret leaned forward to look at Aaron past Jill. "Can we get moving and you two can hash out whose fault it is on the drive? I'll feel better when we put a few miles between lover boy and the bunny boiler, since apparently his lovin' drives women crazy."

"The bunny what?" Jill asked.

Aaron shook his head. "Ignore him. That's Garret's new favorite term."

"Oh." She still didn't understand, but she was too depressed about the situation to care that much.

"Jill."

She glanced up when Aaron said her name. "Yeah?"

"It'll be okay."

"I know. Thanks." She put on a brave face and agreed, but she wasn't all that sure.

She could only hope he was right.

CHAPTER EIGHTEEN

Aaron let go of the handle of Jill's suitcase and juggled the keys on his ring, looking for the one for his apartment. After locating the correct one, he shoved it into the lock and pushed open the door.

Glancing back at Jill, he saw her weariness. "It's getting late. You probably want to go right to sleep. I just have to put some sheets on your bed."

"Don't worry about it. I'll just crash wherever."

"Don't be silly. I've got the open-up sofa and I've got the sheets for it. Just give me one minute to set it up." He grabbed her suitcase and carried it into the apartment. "Come on in, take a seat in the living room and I'll be done before you know it."

"All right." Her tote bag on one shoulder and her carry-on in the other hand, she moved into the apartment barely looking around as he flipped on the lights.

It actually wasn't all that late. It being Sunday, they didn't hit any traffic. He'd made good time on the drive. It probably was more what had happened than the hour that had Jill looking as if every step was an effort.

Aaron felt more horrible with every passing moment. He knew CeCe was a kook, but he'd never guessed how far she'd go.

He shouldn't have lost his patience and told her they were done. Her firing Jill had never crossed his mind. He forced himself to stop worrying about Jill, who was slumped on the sofa with her bag in her lap, and concentrated on making up her bed.

The sheets for the spare room were somewhere in the closet. Probably buried under towels and the two-dozen rolls of toilet paper his mother had picked up for him at the price club where she loved to shop.

Fellow riders crashed with him enough that he was always prepared for guests. Sometimes he was more ready than others. Today, he seemed unable to get anything right.

After taking out the toilet paper and a bath towel, he spotted the sheets. He dumped the toilet paper on the floor and carried the towel to the bathroom. "I'm putting a clean towel in here for you."

"Okay, thank you." She sounded so sad it broke his heart.

Damn CeCe. She was winging her way across the country in her private jet, probably sipping on champagne, and Jill got to crash on the thin mattress with springs from his open-up couch poking her in the back.

Life wasn't fair, but Aaron already knew that. Hell, all bull riders did. Sometimes you covered the ride, sometimes you didn't. Almost always you got thrown in the dirt. The only thing to do was stand up again, dust off and forge ahead.

That was a pretty good inspirational speech he had going in his head as he carried the sheets to the guest room. He'd have to remember it and deliver it to Jill later when she was in the mood to listen.

He made short work of opening the sofa and putting the sheets on the bed. He tossed an extra pillow at the head and a blanket at the foot and was done.

A few beers might make them both feel better. After the scene with CeCe before they'd left today—on top of the entire crazy weekend—he could sure as hell use one.

Hoping he'd remembered correctly and had beer, he

headed for the kitchen and tugged open the fridge.

Jackpot. There was a partially filled six-pack right on the shelf where he'd left it. He didn't bother to ask her. Instead, he just grabbed two longneck bottles from the cardboard holder.

He carried them to the living room and sat on the opposite end of the sofa from where Jill was slumped and looking in a daze.

A lot had happened in a short amount of time. No surprise she was feeling the shock of it all. He twisted one cap off and held the bottle out for her. She took it without comment and pressed it to her lips.

He opened his own bottle and did the same, drawing a long swallow. The cold brew slid down his throat like a balm soothing more than his thirst. He sighed. "This is one weekend I'm glad is over."

"You and me both." Jill cut her gaze to him. "I'm sorry. I'm being selfish and only thinking of myself. I know why I'm happy this weekend is over. Why are you? Because you got hurt today?"

"Um, no. Not quite." He couldn't meet her eyes, but he forced himself to. "I didn't exactly get hurt." Aaron wasn't proud of himself for lying but he'd been desperate.

She frowned. "You didn't?"

"Nope. I pretended I was hurt so I could hide in the medical room for the rest of the event."

"You hid from CeCe?"

"Yup." He hung his head in shame. "That was a real pussy move, I know."

Her laugh had him looking up. "Actually, it was pretty smart."

He smiled. "I can't even take credit for the idea. It was one of the other guys. I just wished it had worked better. She wouldn't give up. She wanted to bring me home to her private masseuse. Said he'd fix me right up. The woman doesn't take no for an answer. I finally had to tell it to her straight. She didn't take it well."

"I know. I walked in on the tail end of it."

"I just hope she doesn't pull her sponsorship over this. The association counts on her money to keep the circuit running."

"So much power over so many people and she really doesn't deserve it. Not any of it. If John Cole had had a better prenup, she'd be nothing but a washed-up, divorced former model." Jill looked at Aaron. "And now I sound like a bitch."

Jill spoke the truth so Aaron shook his head. "No. You don't."

"I really loved the idea of working for a major corporation that was run by a strong woman CEO. But CeCe . . ." Jill let the sentence trail off.

"CeCe isn't that woman." Aaron finished the thought for her.

"Nope. She's not. Not even close." Jill took another pull from the bottle.

Aaron did the same. A comfortable silence based on mutual understanding surrounded them.

Even without talking, Aaron felt close to Jill. It was like they'd been to war together. They'd both battled and survived CeCe. Though Aaron had to think he'd come out of it unscathed compared to the devastation CeCe had made out of Jill's career.

"I'm sorry you got fired over me."

"If it wasn't over this, it would have been something else. I've had a feeling for a while that I was on borrowed time with her anyway. Honestly, Aaron. You can't blame yourself. I don't blame you."

"I'm glad, but I still feel responsible."

"And you're putting me up at your home for the night, so we're even."

"More than the night, Jill. However long you need to get your flight booked, or find another job, or just get your head on straight, you're welcome to stay."

"Thanks."

"My pleasure. Besides, it's nice to have someone to kick back and have a beer with. Ever since Garret and my sister had the baby, I've been kind of on my own."

"Glad I can help." She raised her bottle to him before pressing it to her lips one more time.

Aaron eyed the level in his bottle. "Another one?"

"Sure. Why not? I've got nothing else to do." She lifted one shoulder, looking more relaxed than before.

"That a girl."

His plan was working out nicely.

CHAPTER NINETEEN

Aaron woke from a dead sleep.

Groaning, he rolled over and squinted in the direction of the clock. The red glow of the numbers told him it was too early to be conscious. It was definitely too early to get up. It was still dark outside.

With as tired as he was from the weekend, why he would wake up in the middle of the night, he didn't know. But since he was already awake, he figured he might as well get up and hit the bathroom.

He intended to sleep in tomorrow. With nothing to do until the next event, he could stay in bed as late as he wanted.

Still half asleep, he flipped the covers back and swung his bare feet to the floor. In the boxer shorts he slept in, he stumbled through the apartment he knew so well he didn't need to turn on the lamps.

Down the hall, he saw a strip of light beneath the bathroom door. It was strange that he'd forgotten to turn the bathroom light off before going to bed, but he was too sleepy to worry about it much.

He reached the bathroom door and pushed it open, sucking in a breath at what he saw. Jill sat on the edge of the bathtub, legs spread wide, her hand down the front of her pajama pants. Her eyes had been closed but she opened them at the sound of his intake of breath.

She yanked her hand out of her pants when she saw him standing in the doorway. "Oh, my God. Aaron."

He should have closed the door and backed away, but all he could do was stand there as what he'd walked in on hit him like a sledgehammer.

He'd totally forgotten she was his houseguest. If he'd been fully awake, he would have remembered she was staying with him. Would have realized the bathroom door shouldn't be closed in the middle of the night with the light on unless there was someone inside. But he'd lived alone for years. And he'd had too many beers and too little sleep to be thinking clearly.

"I'm so sorry." Aaron found himself breathing harder at the thought of what Jill had obviously been doing. He didn't move. Neither did she. He should leave. He couldn't bring himself to. "Tell me what to do to."

She swallowed visibly and raised her gaze to meet his. "What do you want to do?"

"I want to come over there to you." Mouth dry, he admitted the truth. At least, he admitted a part of the truth. He didn't tell her everything that was winging through his mind.

What he kept to himself was how he wanted to strip those pants off her and take over what she'd been doing with his own hands and his mouth.

She was breathing as heavily as he was. He watched the outline of her breasts rise and fall beneath the thin cotton of her T-shirt.

"Then do that . . . if you want to." There was an undercurrent of hesitation, uncertainty, in her voice.

Was she really unsure of what he wanted? She needn't have worried.

Aaron didn't need to be asked twice. He was in motion the moment the words were out of her mouth, striding across the small bathroom, closing the short distance between them.

He dropped to his knees in front of her, trying to ignore how his erection tented the front of the too-thin cotton of his boxer shorts.

She didn't ignore it though. He watched her focus drop to the bulge. He itched to touch her, touch himself, to watch her as she watched him doing it, but there was something else he wanted to do first.

Leaning forward, he brushed a hand across her cheek and then cupped the back of her head as he brought his lips to hers. She let out a soft moan at the contact. The sound cut right through him, ratcheting higher his need for her.

Ignoring the soreness in the knee he'd landed on that night, he tipped his head to the side and deepened the kiss, parting her lips with his tongue. She responded with another tiny sound that had him wishing they were in his bed.

They'd both be more comfortable there, but damn, things were moving fast, even for him. He couldn't imagine how she felt. He didn't want to rush her. Or this.

The thick bathroom rug his mother had insisted on buying him cushioned his knee enough he'd be okay. Besides, he was barely aware of anything besides the heat of her mouth and the sound of her breath quickening.

Aaron reached down and ran a fingertip over the seam of her pajama bottoms where it pressed on the juncture of her thighs. She drew in a stuttering breath. He did it again and enjoyed the same reaction.

No woman should ever have to take care of herself when there was a man who was ready, willing and able to do it for her.

Grabbing the waistband of her bottoms with both hands, he wiggled them down over the swell of her hips.

He broke the kiss and watched her face as he did. "This okay?"

Eyes heavily lidded, she didn't protest. Instead, she nodded, braced her palms on the edge of the tub and lifted her hips, giving him the permission and the freedom he needed.

He pulled the bottoms the rest of the way off, all the way past her feet. He tossed them to the floor and ran his hands up the bare skin of her legs, between her thighs and then up higher.

Her breath caught in her throat when he reached her folds and spread her with both thumbs. His hands on her were a beautiful sight. Jill, half naked and breathless, was an even better view. He ran one thumb over her clit. She let out a little gasp.

There was nothing that did him in like the tiny sounds a woman made at times like this. He ran the opposite thumb over her and got the same reaction. Watching her face as he did so, Aaron wet both fingers with his tongue and brought them back to her clit, alternating them in a massage that had Jill dragging in ragged breaths.

An adorable crinkle formed between her brows as she leaned back against the wall, all while focused down so she could watch him work her with his hands.

The muscles of her thighs began to shake. She was close, poised and ready to break into an orgasm. He was breathing as hard as she was as he lowered his head. He replaced his fingers with his mouth and she reacted to the change, letting out a cry and lifting her hips.

He gripped her thighs and worked her faster.

She came apart beneath him, shaking and filling the room with sounds of a woman being well pleased.

He pushed her long and hard until, gasping, she grabbed his head and lifted it off her.

When it was all over, he was bowled over by feelings. Guilt. Doubt. Confusion.

Emotions were something he wasn't usually burdened with in situations such as these. If Jill had been a girl he'd picked up at an event, he'd have already picked her up and tossed her on his bed. He'd bury his aching cock inside her and then order a pizza after he was done, because sex never failed to make him hungry.

Instead, he kneeled on the floor of the bathroom

paralyzed.

This was Jill, not some buckle bunny. She'd worked for the woman he'd spent the weekend in bed with. She'd been fired because of him. Even if it hadn't been his idea to be in bed with CeCe with Jill only one room away, it all still made for an awkward situation.

He shouldn't have touched Jill at all. But damn, he'd enjoyed it while he had been in the moment.

Still perched on the edge of the bathtub, she silently watched him.

For lack of any better idea, he reached for her pants on the floor and handed them to her. "Um, here."

Standing, he noticed the tent in his boxers hadn't gone down at all. In fact, things in that area had gotten worse. Now there was a wet spot in the fabric that accentuated the tip of his hard-on.

As she pulled on her pants, Aaron hooked a thumb toward the doorway. "I'm gonna . . . go."

A frown wrinkled her brow. "Oh."

He paused. Something was up with her. "Unless . . . do we need to talk about this?"

"About that?" Standing, she waved a hand toward the tub—the site of Aaron's mistake—and laughed. "No. I don't want to talk about . . . No." She shook her head.

"Okay. So we're good?" Jeez. It was as if he was some damn teenaged virgin. It was crazy. How had he forgotten how to talk to girls?

At his question, Jill opened her mouth and, looking as if she had no idea what to say, closed it again.

"We're not good." Aaron ran a hand over his face. "I'm so sorry. I shouldn't have done that."

He'd overstepped his bounds. Walking in on her had been bad enough. Invading her privacy like that. But to go over and . . .

What the hell had he been thinking?

She shook her head. "No. That's not the problem."

"Okay. Then what is?" Maybe she was embarrassed.

Hell, he sure would be if the situation were reversed. If she'd walked in on him in the middle of jerking off. He should tell her not to worry. That he'd never seen anything so hot in his life.

"I guess, I thought . . . You know." She lifted one shoulder as her gaze dropped to the bulge in his boxers.

"Oh. Yeah, don't worry about me. That'll go away. Eventually." Yeah, standing in front of her in his underwear while sporting a massive hard-on and having a conversation wasn't embarrassing at all.

"Aaron." She let out a sigh. "I thought maybe we weren't done yet."

Realization hit him. He hadn't wanted to push her into something she didn't want, but maybe she wanted exactly what he did.

Jill knew very well he'd been with CeCe just twenty-four hours ago. He thought that would be a deal breaker for her.

It wasn't for him. CeCe was in his past. With any luck, he'd never have to see or even think about her again, but females were different about this stuff.

A guy could close one door and open the next without looking back. Women—well, he figured they tended to want a bit more distance in between.

"Oh. I didn't want to assume anything. Not knowing what you want . . ." He let the sentence hang in the air, waiting for her to offer.

"You're going to make me say it?" She looked so adorable. All shocked and insulted and, if he wasn't mistaken, interested. In him. That was the best part.

His spirits and hopes lifted as he grinned. "Yeah. I think I am gonna make you say it."

"Aaron." Her voice squeaked with disbelief.

"What?" He took a step toward her and then another. Putting a hand on each of her shoulders, he dropped his forehead until it rested against hers. "Sometimes a guy just likes to hear it, you know?"

She rolled her eyes, obviously catching on that he was

messing with her. "Can I come to bed with you?"

"Is there something wrong with your bed?" He fought the smile as he teased her.

"Yes."

"Really? What? Is the mattress too thin?"

"A little, but it's more that my bed is missing something."

He moved his hands lower on her back, enjoying the warm, soft cotton of her shirt beneath his fingers. He pulled her closer until they were pressed together. "What's it missing?"

Giving her hips a little thrust, she bumped against the bulge in his boxers. "This."

His smile widened. "Oh. Then I suppose you can come to my room since that—" he glanced down between them, "—is standard equipment in my bed."

"Good to hear."

It was very good to hear she wanted him as much as he wanted her.

He'd had about enough of the foreplay in the bathroom when he had a whole apartment to use, but he couldn't resist one more quick kiss. He brought one hand up to cup her face and lowered his mouth to hers.

Even with as tightly as they were clenched together, he couldn't get close enough to her. Not here while vertical.

What little clothing separated them seemed like too much. He craved more contact. So much more. Too much for where they were.

He reached down and hoisted her against him.

Jill wrapped her legs around his back. He carried her out of the bathroom, down the hallway and all the way to his bedroom.

He dropped her onto the mattress and followed her down until he was on top of her on his bed. He kissed her as she wrapped her arms around him, pulling him close and holding him there. Jill captured him in her embrace and he was more than happy to be there.

There was no need to rush. They had all the time in the

world, or at least the rest of the night and all of tomorrow too. He intended to use it all.

The slow, intense kisses she returned in response to his working her mouth told him Jill was in no hurry either. It felt as if they were on the same page, moving at the same speed, just happy to be touching each other.

Kissing her was simple. Easy. Perfect. Being with Jill was the opposite of what being with CeCe had been like.

He hated that he'd even thought CeCe's name while he was with Jill. It felt like a betrayal, but the differences in his feelings about being with Jill were so glaring.

The heat of her palms slid over his bare skin as Jill moved both hands down the muscles of his back. She didn't stop when she reached the waistband of his boxers, but continued the journey down, sliding her hands beneath the fabric.

She snaked one hand around to the front. A more than willing participant in her exploration, Aaron rolled to the side, just enough to give her access.

When she made first contact with him, he hissed in a breath. When she wrapped her hand around him and delivered a single stroke up his length, he couldn't help the moan that rumbled from within him.

He felt her smile beneath his kiss and pulled back an inch. "Feel free to do that move again, if you'd like."

"You enjoyed it, did you?"

"Mmm, hmm." He brushed his lips over her ear and moved down to nip at her throat.

She tipped her head. Her eyes drifted closed as he kissed her neck, but she did as he asked, stroking him at the same time.

He'd intended to take things slow. He really had. But every pass of her hand up and down his length ramped up the need to bury himself in her and finish this.

When she trailed the tip of one finger over his slit, spreading the slick pre-come around the head of his cock, he was done holding back. He pushed his boxer shorts down his legs and tossed them to the floor, leaving him naked as the day he was born on top of the bedcovers.

Jill dropped her gaze to take him in. All of him in.

Seeing her look him over didn't help the urgency to have her. His new goal was to get Jill equally as naked. He went to work to make that happen.

He'd strip her bare, but he would take his time doing it. He started with the bottoms he'd already had off her once tonight. The ones he had foolishly given back to her. He wouldn't make that mistake again.

Now that he knew she was as into this as he was, there'd be no more hesitation on his part.

After tossing the bottoms onto the floor with his own boxer shorts, he moved back to finish the job. He pushed her T-shirt up as he moved his hands up her body, over warm skin, across the soft peaks of her breasts.

He pulled her shirt over her head and flung it, much too intent on Jill to care where it landed. She lay beneath him, bared and beautiful. A feast for the eyes. A feast for his mouth too.

Leaning low, he drew one nipple between his lips while he ran a thumb over the other one. She bowed her back, pressing up toward him. He smiled against her flesh before setting to work to please her more by scraping his teeth over her tender peak.

The reaction made him want her writhing beneath him with him inside her. Then again, he'd be just as happy doing plenty of other things with her, if that's all she could handle right now.

He kneeled on the bed. Watching her face, he ran his hands between her thighs, spreading them wide. He paused, waiting for a signal from her to dictate his next move.

Reaching up, she grabbed his shoulders and guided him closer. As he laid between her legs, she ran her hands down his back. She settled them on his butt cheeks and pulled.

His tip nudged at her entrance. Straightening his arms, he braced above her. "We doing this?"

"I certainly hope so." She frowned. "Don't you want to?"

He laughed that she thought she had to ask. He'd been as hard as a sack of nickels for what had to be half an hour thanks to her. He hadn't thought his willingness was in question.

"Oh yeah. Just making sure."

"I'm very sure." She pulled him closer again.

He felt the wet heat of her body against him. He had to roll off her before he lost his mind, gave in to the temptation and slid into her warmth unprotected.

One unplanned pregnancy in the family was enough. At least his sister and Garret had been married at the time their little *oops* happened. Silver and Garret could take chances. Aaron wasn't going to.

He reached for the bedside table, happy he happened to keep his supply in the bedroom. Not because he brought girls back to his apartment. He really didn't. In fact, Jill was the only one he'd had here besides a girl he'd dated for a few months a couple years ago. But with his mother and sister dropping by to visit all the time, the bedroom drawer seemed like the only private spot to stash something. He didn't trust them not to go snooping in his bathroom cabinets or closet.

The reason didn't matter. He was simply grateful for the close proximity of the condoms now. He didn't have to get out of bed. Didn't have to leave Jill. He only had to reach over and grab one. A quick tear of the foil and he was back right where he wanted to be—between Jill's legs.

Wasting no time to get where he was going, he slid inside her. Her mouth opened as he entered her. He lifted her knees and stroked deeper. She sucked in a breath.

"You okay?" As good as it felt to sink so deep in to this woman, he was worried he'd hurt her.

She laughed. "Yeah. Very okay."

"Good." Because it felt way too good to stop.

Funny that after the initial thrill of being with a sexy older woman had fled, it had taken CeCe's drawer of kinky sex toys to get him excited sexually. That wasn't the case with Jill.

With Jill, all it took was a glimpse of her skin, or the sound of her gasp. A touch. A look. Just . . . her.

He moved inside her and felt a shudder run down his spine like a jolt of electricity surging through him. No batteries. No restraints. No toys necessary. This woman alone was more than enough to thrill him.

Of course, he might not mind exploring some wilder stuff with Jill. One day, but not today.

He loved her until he felt the tingle start inside him, but he wasn't ready to be done yet. He pulled out and concentrated on kissing her until the sensation passed.

When he slid back in, he felt as if he could last for hours. With her, he was in no rush to finish. He had no intention of letting it end anytime soon.

"Jill?"

"Yeah?"

"This might take a while." He leaned back, reached between them and found her clit with his thumb.

She let out a gasp. "That's quite all right. Keep doing that and you can go all night if you want."

He hoped she was serious, because that's exactly what he hoped to do.

CHAPTER TWENTY

Aaron trailed his hand lazily up and down Jill's bare arm. "I'm glad you stayed instead of going to the airport."

Jill lay with her head resting on Aaron's chest, so she heard his incredibly sweet comment as it rumbled through him and against her ear.

"I'm glad too." She was having a much better time with him than she would have waiting at the airport all night for a standby flight.

He angled his head and glanced down at her face. "So, um, wanna tell me what inspired that little self-love session that I walked in on in my bathroom?"

"Oh, God. Aaron, please. Can we never talk about it again?" She hid her face in her hands and tried to roll away from him.

He reached out and grabbed her hip before she could get away and rolled her back. "Nuh, uh. Come on. Tell me."

Finally, she uncovered her eyes and faced him and the embarrassing subject. "I don't know."

"Yeah you do. What made you get out of bed in the middle of the night, go to the bathroom and . . . you know?"

"I couldn't sleep, so I got up to pee. Then when I was there, I went in your medicine cabinet and I smelled your deodorant and then I sniffed your aftershave and that was it."

He lifted his brows high. "The smell of deodorant and aftershave got you horny enough to masturbate?"

"Oh, jeez. Please don't put it like that. I hate both of those words. Oh my God, I'm so embarrassed." She tried to escape again, but he wouldn't let her. When she rolled away from him, Aaron was right behind her.

"Jill, stop being embarrassed right now." He wrapped his arms around her from behind, hugging her against him. With his head resting on hers and his mouth close to her ear, he said, "That is the hottest thing I've ever heard in my life. And seeing you doing it—I swear I could have come right there just from watching you."

"It's still embarrassing."

"Whatever. You'll live. I liked it. A lot. Feel free to do that in front of me anytime."

"Don't hold your breath waiting for that. Okay?"

"We'll see." She felt him smile against her cheek before he kissed her. "What you did led to the best sex of my life, so too bad. If I have anything to say about it, we're doing it again."

Jill let out a harrumph at that. "Right."

"What was that for?" He lifted his head to look down at her.

"I heard you and CeCe together those two nights. And, no, I'm not some kind of creeper eavesdropping. You were just really loud."

"I'm sorry about that. At the time I didn't realize you could hear."

She turned to look at him. "That wasn't my point."

"What is your point?" He didn't seem to be paying attention as he circled her nipple with one finger, but she was going to answer him anyway.

"That you were extremely vocal when you were with her but not with me, so I don't believe for one minute that what we just did was some of the best sex of your life, as you put it. You're just saying that."

"No, I'm not."

"Yes, you are."

He sighed. "Tell me this. Why would I lie to you?"

"To get me in to your bed."

"Too late. I already got you here." He glanced down at their twined legs, tangled together, and then followed his gaze with his hand, running it down her bare skin.

"Yeah, well, getting me into bed was easy because I've been sexually deprived lately. Because I work too many hours. Not because, you know, I can't get a guy." At least that's the excuse she liked to tell herself.

"Whatever the reason, I'm glad for it." He grinned. "Seriously though. I would much rather have been with you the past two nights. You don't know how many times I wished I could have been at the bar with you and everybody else. Or hell, even been able to talk to you at the event without getting nasty looks from CeCe."

"You wished you could talk to me, huh? You did a lot more than talk to CeCe. For such an expensive hotel, the walls were surprisingly thin."

The blood rushed to his cheeks and turned them pink. "Jill . . ." He shook his head. "I don't know what to say."

She shrugged. "There's nothing to say. She's a beautiful woman and you obviously enjoyed the time you two spent together. I'm just saying I didn't hear any sounds like that come out of you tonight, so . . ."

He shook his head. "I didn't want to be there with her. Believe me, after spending about an hour alone with her I'd had enough. I certainly wouldn't have gone back the second night if I could have figured out any way around it."

He didn't have to protest or lie or make excuses. Aaron didn't owe her anything.

"Aaron, really, it's fine. You don't have to say that. Unwilling participants don't make the kind of noise I heard."

"No. Jill. Listen to me." He let out a short laugh. "You can't compare what CeCe did with what you and I did."

"Of course not. There's no comparison. She's a super

model. I'm a marketing geek. She's older with more experience—"

"Jill, no. She had . . . things that she used." He looked as if he regretted his words the moment they left his mouth. "Forget about it. Forget I said anything."

Now this was interesting, and there was no way she was letting him get away without explaining the comment.

"Oh, no." She lifted up on one elbow. "What kind of *things* did she use?"

He drew in a breath and let it out through his nose, his lips pressed tightly together as if he didn't want to talk.

"Aaron. Come on. You can't say something like that and not explain."

"It's nothing. She just had toys and stuff."

Shock had Jill widening her eyes. She tried to reconcile the kinky woman who'd used sexual paraphernalia on Aaron until he'd wailed like a banshee with the self-indulgent woman who didn't like to get her hands dirty.

"Sex toys? CeCe? Wait. She travels with that stuff?"

"Apparently, she ordered and had it delivered just for me." He rolled his eyes.

"Holy shit. I never would have guessed." She couldn't have been more shocked.

Though, when she thought about it, CeCe did like to be bossy. Jill could totally see her as a dominatrix.

He let out a snort. "No shit. Me either."

Now that Jill knew what had Aaron shouting so loudly she'd heard him from two rooms away, she was a little jealous. She wanted that reaction for herself.

She sat up, intent on getting more details. "So, exactly what kind of toys are we talking here?"

"No." He shook his head. "We're not talking about this."

"Why not? I think I'd like to see some of these toys. Maybe pick up a few for myself to try."

"No."

"But—"

"No," he repeated, more emphatically.

"Fine. But you certainly sounded as if you enjoyed it."

"I'll show you what I enjoy." He rolled on top of her and pressed his mouth to hers, cutting off any further discussion on this topic.

That was fine, for now. CeCe had gotten to Aaron first, but Jill was with him now, and judging by the hard-on she felt pressing between her thighs, he was ready to make love to her without any assistance, battery-operated or other. Jill felt a certain satisfaction knowing that.

Yes, they'd have to get back to the real world eventually, but not tonight, and not for the next couple of weeks.

That was plenty of time for her to get acquainted with every little thing that Aaron liked and the things that made him lose control.

Jill liked that idea a lot.

CHAPTER TWENTY-ONE

The first thing Aaron was conscious of was a buzzing near his head.

As he woke further, a barrage of other realizations hit him. The warm soft body he lay pressed against. The sound of Jill's steady breathing as she slept. The hard-on that nestled between him and her.

Enough light streamed into the room from behind the blinds for him to realize it must be morning, if not late morning. Whoever was disturbing him by calling his cell phone had probably assumed he'd be awake already. He would have been if he hadn't been up half the night.

No regrets there. He'd gladly trade sleep for a night spent with Jill.

Trying not to disturb her, he turned as best he could while leaving his arm beneath her head. He stretched for the cell on the nightstand. Finally, he connected with the phone.

Grabbing it, he squinted at the readout. With tired eyes that he couldn't seem to focus yet, he made out the blurred name.

Garret.

That call could wait until later. His sister had already had the baby, so the family wasn't on labor alert day and night any longer. If there was anything wrong or really important, Garret would send a text. Aaron hit to dismiss the call and let it go to voicemail, then set the phone back on the nightstand.

Lying still, he heard Jill still breathing, soft and slow. Happy he hadn't woken her and they could both hide in bed a bit longer, he snuggled deeper beneath the covers against her body.

Behind him, his phone buzzed twice and he smothered a cuss. That was his text-message alert. He had to look and make sure there was no emergency.

Letting out a sigh, he reached one more time for the cell. One-handed, he navigated to the text. Reading it, he realized there was nothing wrong at all. It was just his brother-in-law being nosy asking how his hot night with Jill had been.

Knowing Garret, he'd meant it as a joke. Little did his friend know Aaron had a hell of a night with Jill, followed by what could turn out to be one hell of a day if Aaron had his way.

That thought had him dropping the cell back onto the nightstand and reaching for Jill. He'd gotten a look at the clock. It wasn't that early, and parts of him were very awake. He didn't see any harm in delivering a gentle nudge to his bed companion.

Hell, he couldn't think of a better way to be woken up himself. He hoped Jill agreed.

The tiniest motion, just a tip of his hips, pressed his erection between her legs. He closed his eyes and enjoyed the friction. He'd like to bury his cock somewhere else, and he'd get to that, but this would do for the moment.

Days off were made for nice, slow morning sex.

She moaned and snuggled closer to him, "Was that your cell phone?"

"Yeah. Garret being nosy. Wants to know what we're doing. I'm ignoring him." Aaron angled his stroke and moved closer to his ultimate destination, rubbing the head of his cock between her warm soft lips.

"We can't stay in bed all day doing this, you know." Her

words made him smile, even if she was completely wrong.

"Not so. We definitely can and should do this all day long." But they didn't have to stay in bed to do it. He had an entire apartment at his disposal and he intended to take advantage of that.

"We did it for so long last night it feels like I have a nest of knots in my hair." She reached up and ran a hand over the back of her head.

That tidbit filled him with a purely masculine sense of pride. "Don't bother trying to fix your hair now. I'm just gonna mess it up again."

"You think so, do you?" she asked.

"I do. Why not? You have something else you need to do instead?" He nuzzled beneath her hair, running his tongue along the whorls of her ear. He felt her shudder in response.

Jill drew in a breath. "No, nothing else to do."

"Good, and I have nothing to do today . . . except for you." He grabbed her chin and angled her face towards him.

Aaron covered her lips with his and slid his tongue into her mouth while pushing his cock between her legs. He broke the kiss. "I'm gonna put on a condom."

"Okay." Her response was soft and sleepy even while filled with need.

Smiling that there were no more arguments from her he slid the latex on and pushed inside with slow, deep, lazy strokes that proved he had no plans to rush this. He could very happily do this all day, taking only short breaks for sustenance and to rehydrate.

"Warning you." He paused to groan as she clenched around him. "Mornings can take me a while."

She tilted her head to look at him. "Longer than last night?"

"Yup. You complaining?" Reaching down, he pressed two fingers against her clit and felt her hips jerk forward.

She hissed in a breath. "No."

"Good." He'd make her come like this, with him inside her. Then maybe they'd take a shower together. He'd been thinking about having his hands all over her slick, soapy skin. *Mmm.*

At some point, he wanted to run his mouth over every inch of her. Hopefully, she'd do the same to him.

The image of her taking him in her mouth had his body clenching in anticipation. Yup. Aaron could definitely fill an entire day with exploring Jill and never grow bored. Not even close.

But right now he had to concentrate. He wanted to absorb every nuance. Listen to the hitch in her breath every time he bottomed out inside her. Feel the tremor in her muscles as she tensed her thighs. Enjoy the tightening of her body around his as she primed for release. All from nothing more than the lazy rocking of his hips and the gentle circling of his fingers on her.

No toys. No restraints.

Just a man and a woman and a bed, and he couldn't be happier, especially when he felt Jill start to come around him.

His kiss muffled her soft cries as she bucked against his hand. He needed to convince her to stay with him for his break and not fly home sooner. He'd have to keep her in a sex haze night and day.

How hard could it be? Hell, he'd been in one since he'd walked in on her in the bathroom and he didn't see it changing any time soon.

Her pulses slowed as she finished coming around him. She felt boneless in his hands as he rolled her onto her stomach. He shoved a pillow beneath her hips, propping her up before he thrust inside from behind.

"I'm gonna finish this, then I'm gonna go down on you for like an hour." He spoke as he plunged inside her. Her breathing was coming in gasps as he continued with what he wanted them to do. "Then I want your mouth on me. And then we're going to do it all over again."

He was breathing pretty hard himself as the room seemed to grow hotter around him.

Aaron leaned low, close to her ear. "That all right with

you?"

She nodded.

"Good." He was done with talking for now.

Aaron thrust fast and hard. Slick with sweat from his exertion, he felt the end coming. He held deep and came with a loud groan.

Finally, Jill angled her head. From where he braced above her on shaking arms, he could see the side of her face as she gasped. "Are you always this insatiable?"

It took more energy than he had at the moment to let out a short laugh.

Little did she know he was usually a one-and-done kind of guy. Finish, say goodbye and not see the girl again. It had been a long time since he'd been with a woman he wanted to spend the day with after having spent the night with her.

Hell, he wanted to spend the next two weeks with her. It was with complete sincerity that he could answer her, "No."

"Not even with CeCe?"

He heard the darkness in her voice. If he accomplished nothing else, he was going to get Jill to stop comparing herself to CeCe. Even better, he'd love to get her to forget all about that woman and the huge mistake of last weekend.

Aaron rolled her over so he could speak directly to her, face-to-face. "Baby, I couldn't get away from her fast enough, and you know that."

A tiny smile tipped up the corner of her mouth. "Yeah, I know. I was the keeper of the big-boy truck keys. Remember?"

"Yes, you were. And if you're lucky, maybe I'll take you for a ride in that big-boy truck again." Much later.

Right now, he couldn't think of a thing that would make him want to leave the apartment and venture out into the real world.

His phone vibrated again, signaling the arrival of a new text, and he sighed.

"Maybe you should see what they want."

Aaron pouted. "I don't want to."

She rolled her eyes, shaming him into reaching for the phone. He remained straddling her legs so she couldn't sneak away as he opened the text.

"It's just Garret again. He and my sister want us to come for dinner tonight." Aaron started punching in a reply.

"What are you telling him?" she asked.

"No."

"No? Why?"

"Because I don't want to." That excuse hadn't worked before when he hadn't wanted to check the text and she'd made him to it anyway, but he figured it was worth a try. One look at her deep scowl told him it had failed again. Sighing, he deleted what he'd written and started over. He glanced at Jill. "You sure you want to spend all that time with my family?"

"Yes. I like Garret and I can't wait to meet Silver and the baby." She seemed far more excited about it than him.

"Okay. Fine. I'll tell him yes, but don't say I didn't warn you." He teased, but deep down he loved how Jill fit so seamlessly into his life.

She was easy and fun and the sex . . . he couldn't think too much more about that or he'd never get out of bed and to the shower they both needed after this last sweaty bout.

He hit send on the text and tossed the phone on to the nightstand again. Standing, he reached for her hand and pulled her upright.

"Come on. Time for our shower." He waggled his eyebrows.

She laughed. "Aren't you tired yet?"

"It's just a shower, Jill. Jeez. One track mind much?" Pulling her naked toward the bathroom, he smiled.

Yup. Just a shower, where he'd have his hands on every inch of her soapy body. He knew exactly where all that would lead.

Good thing he'd texted Garret that they wouldn't be over until much, much later.

CHAPTER TWENTY-TWO

"So how's it going? Are you home?" Jackie asked.

"Not exactly."

"Flight delays?" Her sister's voice was ripe with sympathy. "Ugh, that sucks. I hate delays, but I thought flying in the private jet you'd avoid all that. Was it weather related?"

Jill had to stop her sister's outpouring of sympathy. It only made her feel worse about the whole situation. "I got fired."

"What?"

"CeCe flipped out, fired me, took the limo to the private jet and left me stranded with my luggage in the parking lot of the arena."

"Oh my God. That's unbelievable."

"No kidding." Jill was having trouble believing it herself.

"So what did you do?"

"A couple of the bull riders were nice enough to give me a ride."

"So you're waiting on a standby flight?"

"Um. No."

"Jill, where are you and what are you doing?"

"At the moment, I'm in North Carolina." The second question was less easy to answer. What Jill was doing was having amazing sex with Aaron day and night, but she couldn't say that. "I'm crashing at a friend's place."

"What friend?"

"One I met at the bull rides."

"And this friend's name is?" Jackie sounded a bit too interested.

"Aaron." Jill braced herself for her sister's reaction.

Jackie didn't disappoint as she squealed into the phone. "You're staying with a bull rider?"

"Uh, yeah, he's a bull rider."

"Oh my God. You had sex with him."

"What?" How in the world could Jackie know that? She couldn't. It was obviously just a shot in the dark. "I never said that."

"You didn't have to. I can hear it in your voice."

"You can not."

"Go ahead. Deny it. Tell me you haven't."

"I can't." Jill scrunched up her face. This was a no-win situation. She hated the idea of admitting it to her sister even more than she hated lying to her.

There was another high-pitched squeal. "Tell me everything."

"I will not." Jill glanced at the door of the guest room.

She had spent the better part of the day either naked or in Aaron's T-shirt, but he had finally left her alone long enough for her to sift through her luggage and find something to wear for dinner. That didn't mean he wasn't within earshot. The last thing she wanted him to overhear was her telling Jackie about their private time together.

"Come on. Give me something here so I can live vicariously through you. Is he cute?"

"Yes. Very."

"Details. Eyes. Hair. Height. Penis size."

"Jackie!" Jill couldn't help but laugh.

"Come on. Spill."

The truth was she was dying to talk to somebody about Aaron, so her sister didn't have to push too hard.

"Okay. He's got these gorgeous eyes. I can't even describe

the color. It's so blue that it's almost indigo. And his hair is brown so it sets off the color of his eyes and makes them look even bluer, and he's tall and, oh my God, he's in such good shape. All the bull riders are. I mean they have to be."

Jill realized she was babbling and stopped. It took a second or two, but finally Jackie said, "Wow. You really like this guy."

"Well, yeah. I mean he's nice and he's sweet enough to let me stay here until I can get a flight home that won't cost me an arm and a leg." Jill realized she hadn't gotten around to booking a flight today. She'd have to do that before they left for dinner.

Funny, she wasn't in such a hurry to get back to California as she had been.

"You know, since you're looking for a new job anyway, why don't you look on the East Coast? You could be closer to me and Mom and Dad. And closer to your hottie bull rider . . ."

"Let's not jump the gun on that last part." Jill was very aware of the kind of life Aaron lived. She'd seen it firsthand.

He'd gone from being in bed with CeCe to being in bed with her the next night. She wasn't naïve enough to think that kind of thing was an oddity for him.

There were females who hunted professional cowboys like it was a sport. And Aaron, with as good as he looked and as well as he ranked, would be a prized trophy for many.

It was all too much to think about. Best to just enjoy this time. Take it for what it was and no more.

Jill realized her sister was being very quiet. "Jackie, you there?"

"Yeah, I'm here. I'm just waiting for you to let yourself like a guy for once instead of running away."

"I don't do that."

"Yeah, you do."

"Look, I have to get moving. We're having dinner at his sister's house."

"You're having dinner with his family?" Jackie's shock was

clear.

"Don't get excited about that either. It's not like I'm meeting his parents. His sister is married to one of the bull riders I know. It's no big deal."

"Uh, huh." Jackie's comment was tinged with skepticism

Jill sighed. "Okay, enough. Think whatever you want. I need to get changed. Just do me a favor? Don't tell Mom and Dad I got fired. I don't want them to worry. I'll tell them, but not yet. I'd like to have something else lined up before I do."

"All right. I won't tell, if you promise to at least look for jobs near here. If you won't do it for your love life, do it for me. I miss you."

"I miss you too. And I promise."

"Okay. Then I'll let you go get ready for your date with the cowboy and his family. Talk tomorrow. Bye."

"It's not a date—" Jill's protest came too late as her sister disconnected.

She tossed the phone down and turned to her suitcase.

"It's not a date." She repeated it aloud to remind herself of that fact.

This was all just fun. She needed to remember that. She was leaving, and he was going back on the circuit. That was it. Just this.

A stupid, ill-advised hope niggled at the back of her brain that this might be more. Thinking like that was a good way to get hurt.

Mad at herself for letting Jackie make her start thinking things she shouldn't, Jill tossed her clothes from one side of the suitcase to the other searching for what, she didn't know.

It was just dinner with Aaron and Garret, Silver and their baby. No big deal.

Yeah, right.

CHAPTER TWENTY-THREE

Aaron cracked open the bottle of beer and drew in a long swallow as Garret watched him. "You not talking? Again?"

High flames licking over the burgers on the barbecue caught Aaron's attention. He tipped a chin toward the grill. "I think you'd better move those to the upper rack before they burn."

"Don't change the subject." Metal spatula in hand, Garret glanced back at Aaron as he transferred the meat patties one by one.

It seemed as if the only thing Garret did lately was interrogate Aaron for information about his sex life. He must really be bored, even though it seemed as if the baby kept both parents running twenty-four/seven.

"Nothing to talk about, dude."

"That's what you said last time. Right before CeCe Cole had you hiding rather than being her bitch."

"I was never CeCe Cole's bitch." As he said them, the words rang hollow in Aaron's ears.

With all the meat safely away from the flames, Garret put the spatula down and turned to face Aaron. "All right, let's move away from that subject and on to the current girl in your life."

Aaron glanced at the house to make sure his sister and Jill were still in the kitchen and not anywhere where they could hear this conversation. "Will you please stop? You know as well as I do why Jill is staying at my place."

"Yup." Garret nodded. "The jealous bunny boiler fired her because of you."

With friends like Garret, Aaron didn't need enemies. And he was ready to kill Mustang for telling Garret about that damn bunny-killer movie.

"Listen up, because I'm gonna say this one time and one time only." Aaron paused, and when Garret looked as if he might actually keep quiet and listen, he continued, "She's going back to California as soon as she can find a cheap flight. Until then, she's crashing at my place where you know very well I have a guest bed since you've slept there yourself."

All of that was true. He did have a guest bed, even if Jill had spent half the night and the day in Aaron's bed with him.

"And after she flies home to California, then what?"

"Then she'll look for a new job, I guess." Aaron shrugged, but the guilt over the unintentional part he'd played in Jill's firing twisted his gut.

"I'm not talking about her job. I'm asking if you two are going to keep in touch."

"I don't know. Why do we have to talk about this?" Aaron shot another look in the direction of the back door.

"Because judging by the way the two of you keep staring at each other, I'm thinking that you like her and she likes you."

"I like lots of people. You used to be one of them." Joking seemed Aaron's best defense against this subject he didn't want to discuss.

"That's not what I mean, and you know it."

"And we're not in middle school where I have to ask you to pass a note to her in study hall to see who likes who."

"You sure about that?" Garret cocked a brow.

"Very sure. And don't burn my burger. You know I like it bloody in the middle."

"No can do. Silver says no more rare burgers. It's too dangerous. Medium to well-done only."

Aaron widened his eyes. "I don't give a fuck what my sister says."

Garret clucked his tongue. "No more cussing either. Silver doesn't want the baby to hear those kinds of words."

"Are you kidding?"

"Nope."

"The baby can't even crawl yet, never mind talk."

Garret shrugged. "That's what she wants, so that's what we do."

What the hell had happened to his leather-wearing Harley-riding sister to make her turn a complete one-eighty? Aaron knew the answer to that. The baby had happened.

And Garret—the guy who'd used to party as hard as anyone—had done a complete turnaround right along with her.

If this was what marriage did to people, changed them beyond recognition, then they could have it. Aaron was happy being single.

"So after the break, the next event is in California . . ." Garret stared at the rapidly cooking burgers as he let that suggestive tidbit hang in the air.

"Yeah?" Aaron played dumb when he knew very well what Garret was trying to hint at. That he could see Jill while he was there. He wasn't about to give Garret that satisfaction, even if the thought had crossed his mind.

And if he did visit her, what would that accomplish? Get him attached to someone who lived thousands of miles away? Make him become domesticated like Garret had?

The back door opened and out stepped Jill and his sister with the baby on her hip.

Garret grinned and moved to give the baby a kiss on the cheek and then Silver one on the mouth. "Almost done here, baby."

"Good. Table's all set and the salad made." Silver looked as happy as Garret did, just over some barbecued meat.

Though Aaron knew their bliss came from more than the hamburgers Garret was ruining.

Aaron's gaze shot to Jill. She was smiling as she watched Garret tickle the baby in Silver's arms. Maybe domesticated life wasn't so horrible after all.

Jill turned to Aaron and he had to pretend that he hadn't been staring at her. He raised his beer to his mouth and took a swallow, acting casual as she walked toward him.

"So good news."

"Yeah? What?" he asked.

"Silver told me about this website that sells last-minute plane tickets for really cheap. I guess the airlines would rather discount fares than fly with empty seats. Anyway, I used her computer and I got a ticket for a great price."

"Really? Great. So when are you flying?"

"Tomorrow. Isn't that crazy? It was less than the tickets I was looking at for next week."

Tomorrow. Aaron had to wrap his head around that.

More than twelve straight hours of sex with this woman and he still hadn't had his fill of her if the disappointment that flooded him at the thought of her leaving was any indication.

It seemed as if they were just starting to get to know each other better and she was flying away.

"Wow. What time? I'll drive you to the airport."

"It's kind of early, I'm afraid. It's a nine a.m. flight, so I need to get there and check my bag by eight, I figure."

"That's fine. I'll take you."

"Thank you. I really appreciate it."

"No problem at all. My pleasure." That last part was a lie. Aaron realized he'd rather do just about anything than help Jill leave.

Damn.

CHAPTER TWENTY-FOUR

It was full dark by the time they walked into Aaron's apartment after dinner at Garret's place.

"I'd better get to my room and pack." Jill hooked a thumb toward the door to the guestroom. "I want everything ready tonight since we're leaving for the airport early in the morning."

"Good idea." Aaron nodded even though he thought a far better idea would be Jill in his bed.

She turned and headed through the doorway, leaving Aaron frowning in the hall, unhappy she was leaving so soon and really unhappy that she was in her own room and not in his.

Packing. *Pfft.*

He spent half his life on the road traveling to venues. He knew damn well what it took. All she had to do was toss her stuff in her bag and zip it up.

As he went to the bathroom to brush and floss his teeth, his mind raced. Was she going to get done what she needed to do and then come to him?

He took his time getting ready for bed, stalling while hoping she'd make an appearance. He'd already taken off the clothes he'd worn to dinner and pulled on boxer shorts to sleep in, but she still hadn't come looking for him.

Aaron lost his patience. Waiting around for something to happen wasn't for him. Taking action was.

He strode down the hall, barefoot and shirtless. Her door was open. He could see her inside. He stopped in the hallway and watched her.

Wearing nothing but a long T-shirt, she stood in front of her suitcase and stared at the neatly folded clothes.

"All done?" he asked. At his question, she glanced up.

"I think so. My clothes for tomorrow are laid out. I'll just throw what I'm wearing now and my toiletry bag in the suitcase in the morning. I even plugged in my phone and tablet and computer, so they'll all be fully charged for the plane ride." She laughed but it sounded sad. "Not that I have any work to do. Maybe I can brush up my resumé. Or hell, I might even read a book and relax."

Jill had said she was done packing, so he didn't feel at all guilty as he took the few steps to cover the distance between them. He drew her into his arms. She looked as if she needed it.

"I think that all sounds like a very good idea." He pulled her closer against him. "For tomorrow. For tonight, I have a few ideas of my own."

"Yeah?" She looked up at him.

"Yeah." Aaron dipped his head and covered her mouth with his. He wasn't taking any chances by allowing her an opportunity to talk. She might come up with some bullshit excuse why they shouldn't do this.

A couple of reasons why he shouldn't kiss her now careened into his head as he worked her mouth with his . . . They should both get a good night's sleep. They probably shouldn't get any more involved with each other since she was leaving.

He kept kissing her anyway, confident she wouldn't ask him to stop. He staked his claim, sliding his tongue against hers while moving his hands down to clamp her body tightly against his.

His need overtook his patience and he broke the kiss. "Come to my room."

Eyes heavily lidded as she opened them to look up at him, Jill nodded. "Okay."

That was all Aaron needed to hear. He crashed his mouth against hers for one more quick, hard kiss before he grabbed her hand. He pulled her down the hall to his room.

This was no time for hesitation. They were counting the time until she left in hours now, not days.

This time tomorrow, she'd be at her place and he'd be at his, and there would be no chance to make up for regrets.

Aaron had no intention of lying in his bed alone tomorrow night and wishing they'd spent one last night together. She was here now. He wasn't going to squander this time.

One glance at Jill's expression told Aaron she was rethinking being with him tonight.

Fuck that. They could both second-guess this in the morning, but he'd be damned if he let her worry about it now. Not when it was so easy to distract her.

Aaron ran one hand beneath the bottom of her T-shirt and connected with the bare skin of her thigh. He moved up from there, traveling until he hit where he wanted to be.

He slid one finger into the warmth at the juncture of her thighs and groaned. He stayed there for a moment, circling the tight bundle of nerves.

Watching as a frown creased her brow as she closed her eyes, he had a feeling she was still thinking. He could stop that.

Increasing the speed with which he worked her had her breath quickening. He braced his free hand on her lower back as she started to shake. He wanted to kiss her, but he wanted something else more. To hear her come and to watch her face as she did.

It was worth the wait when Jill finally let go, clinging to his shoulders with both hands. Her eyes squeezed shut tightly while she cried out.

Any other day, he would have gentled his touch and brought her down slowly. Today, he was too damn worked up and, yes, needy from knowing she'd be gone soon.

He lifted her and tossed her onto the mattress. She landed with a squeal and a bounce as he strode around the bed to the nightstand. After sliding on a condom with record-breaking speed, he was back to Jill.

He wasted no time getting where he needed to be. Inside her.

She was more than ready for him. He slid into her slick heat easily. One push had him fully seated inside her and surrounded by her heat. He didn't play any games to make it last longer like he had during their first time together.

This time, a feral urge had him needing to finish this. Like it would mark her as his. It was crazy, he knew that, but when he felt his body nearing completion, he sped up. He pounded into Jill until he came with a force that had him shaking with aftershocks even after it was done and he collapsed over her.

Aaron was surrounded by the combined sounds of their breathing and the pounding of her heart beneath him as he lay on her breast.

He opened his eyes and lazily ran a thumb over her nipple. He watched it tighten and pucker beneath his touch. "Sleep in here tonight . . . please?"

"Okay."

Her assurance eased his mind. This hadn't been their last time together. He had all night, and he was going to take advantage of it.

CHAPTER TWENTY-FIVE

Concentration was futile.

Jill sat in her tiny seat on the airplane and hit the button to put her tablet to sleep. The ebook she'd been trying to read wasn't holding her concentration. No fault of the author. Jill had simply forgotten how to relax.

She'd worked on her resumé for a bit when they'd first taken off, but she wasn't all that inspired. Besides, not all that much had changed in the two years since she'd gotten—and lost—the job at Cole.

All she would have to do is add the dates of her employment and job description and she'd be done and ready to send it out to potential employers. Well, that and come up with an excuse as to why she'd left the position without a reference. *My boss was crazy* probably wouldn't fly in an interview.

Maybe she should look for work on the East Coast closer to her family, like Jackie had suggested.

Jill hated that the next thought to follow was that it would also put her closer to Aaron. She knew too much about the professional bull-riding circuit to think this fling with Aaron could lead anywhere except to heartache for her.

He was too busy traveling around the country and being

with a different girl every night . . . or at least every two nights.

Static sounded before the voice of the flight attendant took over, advising the passengers that they'd be landing shortly and they should begin to stow all their carry-on belongings again.

Jill drew in a breath. She was almost home. Home, where she'd walk into a dark apartment and sleep in an empty bed.

She was so mentally and physically exhausted from everything that had happened and from Aaron waking her up twice during the night, she was in no position to be brave and move ahead today.

Tomorrow, after a good night's sleep, she'd be in a better state of mind to be strong and bravely face the future. She'd allow herself one night to pine over him. No more.

The fact he'd entered his cell phone number into her phone wasn't going to help her forget about him or the weekend. He'd said it was in case her flight got canceled or she got bumped. She could call him and he'd come back and get her.

Even as she thought how she should delete the number, she knew she wouldn't.

She had been better off in the middle of her dry spell. Sex complicated everything. At least for her it did. Did it for men? For Aaron? Sadly, she doubted it.

Pushing all thoughts of him out of her head, Jill planned the rest of her journey. After they landed she'd have to grab the suitcase she'd checked from baggage claim then head outside to find a taxi to take her home since she no longer had access to the Cole car service account.

Damn CeCe. And damn John Cole too for cheating on her, or at least for not having a better prenuptial agreement so his ex-wife wouldn't get the crown jewel in his corporate empire where she'd have the power to fire Jill. All because she'd dared to talk to or glance at Aaron.

Anger replaced sadness. Jill preferred that. It fueled her. Provided incentive to move on from this to something even better than her crappy old job.

With that in mind, Jill started to look forward to looking for a new job. The next step in what would be a bright future. Maybe CeCe had done her a favor. Either way, Jill was going to make the best of a bad situation.

The best revenge was success.

Jill's new bright attitude lasted through the plane landing at LAX, all the way through baggage claim and to her hailing a taxi. She was slightly less enthusiastic about her future in the cab when she realized what the ride from the airport to her apartment was going to cost, but there was nothing she could do about it.

Once settled in the backseat and on the way home, Jill found her cell phone in her carry-on and powered it on.

Messages flooded her inbox and had the phone doing a little jig as it vibrated in her hand with text alerts.

Two were from her sister, asking if she'd landed yet and demanding she call when she was home safely no matter what the time. The third text message was from Jill's coworker— make that *former* coworker.

Jill opened it and read, *"What the hell happened this weekend? Call me!"*

She didn't want to put Mary in the bad position of asking what was going on while she was still at work, but Jill couldn't wait for the work day to be over. She dialed Mary's cell number rather than her desk.

Mary answered on the second ring.

"Hey. It's Jill. I just got your message. What's going on?"

Mary let out a snort. "You tell me. All I know is you and CeCe left for the bull rides last Friday. She took Monday off and then this morning she came in like a bitch on heels. Yelling, ranting. She had the finance department cut all the sponsorship money for the bull-riding organization out of the annual budget for next year. Then she announced you no longer worked for the company and asked me to clean out your desk."

Shit. This whole mess with CeCe and Aaron and Jill had

blown up way out of proportion. Now it affected hundreds of people. Thousands if she counted the fans who attended the events.

Cole was a huge contributor. Without that money, what would happen? Did the organization have enough operating cash to run future events?

"Did she say anything else? Like why?" Was CeCe bad mouthing Jill or Aaron all over the company?

"No. That's why I'm asking you."

It made sense. CeCe wouldn't want anyone to know her hot young lover had turned down her offer to fly home with her. That would be embarrassing. And since CeCe was crazy enough to believe Aaron had turned her down because of Jill, she wouldn't mention her either.

Still, the situation remained the same. She'd pulled the sponsorship money. What the hell was going to happen now?

Jill didn't know. "Um, I don't know. She let me go, so I flew back on my own."

"You have no idea why she fired you or why she broke off the sponsorship?"

"No, besides the fact she's crazy."

Mary snorted. "Well, yeah. That we know. But nothing specific triggered her?"

"Not that I can think of." No way Jill could tell Mary the truth and risk CeCe's wrath if word got out. She could ruin any future career prospects. "I'll make a few phone calls and see if I can find out anything."

"Okay. Call me if you do."

"I will. Bye."

Jill was going to make a phone call all right, but not for the reason she'd told Mary. She had to let Aaron know what had happened, if he didn't know already.

CHAPTER TWENTY-SIX

Aaron flipped through the channels on the television.

How many hundreds of stations were there now? And still it seemed as if there was nothing on. At least nothing that could hold his attention. Or keep his mind off wondering what Jill was doing.

He glanced at the time on his cell phone. She'd probably have landed by now. Yet there was no text from her. Not that there should be. She'd never promised she would let him know that she'd arrived safely.

Still, it would be nice if she did. They'd spent two nights tangled up together in his bed. He'd think the least she'd do was text and say she was home.

He found himself scowling more at himself and his own behavior than at Jill or hers. He was acting like some silly love-struck girl, getting all twisted because he didn't get a call.

Restless, he aimed the remote control at the television again and started to flip through the shows on Netflix while wondering why he was still paying for cable when there was nothing on to watch.

His cell vibrating next to him on the cushion had him tossing the remote down as he grabbed for the phone.

It was Garret. Pissed at himself for being disappointed it

wasn't Jill calling, Aaron answered. "Hey."

"Hey. What are you up to?"

"Nothing. Just sitting here. Watching TV."

"I'm watching the game. Why don't you come over here?"

"So I can sit there and do the same thing as I'm doing here?"

"Yeah. Why not?" Garret asked.

Because Aaron was already settled in where he was and there he would have to wear pants, while in his own place he could stay in boxer shorts.

Of course, he was also bored and sick of his own company. It was going to be a long break between competitions if he didn't get over this restlessness.

With a sigh, he hoisted himself off the cushion. "Okay. I'll be there in ten."

"Great. I just ordered a pizza."

Even better. Maybe Aaron could eat his way out of this funk. Christ, he really was acting like a girl. "All right. See you in a few."

Aaron pulled jeans on right over his boxers and slid boots on over the socks he already had on. He didn't bother changing the T-shirt he was wearing. It seemed like too much effort to dig in the drawer for another. His shirt was moderately clean. It was good enough anyway. He was only going to see relatives.

After he grabbed his cell and his keys, he headed to the truck.

He pulled in the drive of Garret and his sister's place in a few minutes, as promised. Sometimes it was handy they'd moved so close. Other times—like when his sister popped in unannounced and uninvited—not so much.

The front door was unlocked like it usually was. Aaron didn't bother knocking.

"Hey. I'm here." He walked in and made a general announcement to anyone in hearing distance as he did.

"*Shh.*" Silver popped out of one of the bedrooms, wide-eyed. She pulled the door closed behind her and came to him.

"I just got the baby down."

"Oh, sorry." Aaron cringed. He kept forgetting there was now a little one to worry about. "Garret in the living room?"

"Yeah. Watching the game and eating pizza. There better be some left. I'm starving."

Aaron silently agreed. He hadn't realized he was hungry until hearing the word pizza. Now that he had, he was dying for some.

"I heard that and there's plenty. I ordered a large. Jeez. How much do you think I eat?" Slice in hand, Garret sat on the sofa with the closed box in front of him on the coffee table. He frowned at the doorway.

"The answer to that question is *a lot.*" Aaron laughed, feeling lighter already now that he was with people, ready to kick back, watch the game, eat some pizza, maybe have a beer if Garret had any. Yeah. This was good.

It was good he got out of the apartment. Being cooped up alone had to be what had him feeling so out of sorts. He was used to traveling. Having nothing to do, no place to be, was getting to him.

His cell vibrated in his pocket. He jumped to pull it out thinking that—even though he'd vowed to put her out of his head—it might be Jill.

One look at the read out and the unfamiliar area code told him that it very well could be her. Holy shit.

He hit to answer. "Hello?"

"Aaron? It's me. Jill."

He knew it was Jill before she'd added her name. He'd know that voice anywhere. After hearing her breathe his name in the dark while he loved her, how could he not?

Silver and Garret were both sitting in the living room attacking the pizza. He didn't need an audience for this call with Jill.

Heart pounding, Aaron wandered back into the hall.

Jill had called him and a real phone call too, not just a text. He loved that she'd done that.

"Hey. I see you got home safely."

"Um, yeah. Well, I'm not quite home. I'm in the taxi from the airport. I didn't want to wait to call you."

She didn't want to wait to call him. Those words had him smiling. "I'm glad."

"You might not be glad when you hear why."

"Why? What's wrong?" If he hadn't been so damned happy about her contacting him the moment she landed in California, he might have noticed sooner that there was a strange tone in her voice.

"I got some news from a former coworker of mine at Cole Shocks."

"Okay." The mention of Cole of course brought to mind CeCe. Aaron knew this couldn't be good.

"CeCe pulled the sponsorship money when she got to work this morning. She's no longer supporting your organization." Jill delivered the bad news in a rush of words.

What she said had him reaching out to brace one palm against the wall. He'd been concerned that this could happen, but he'd never honestly thought it would.

Shit. What was he going to do?

"This morning?" His mind spun trying to comprehend what had happened and the ramifications of it.

It was amazing he hadn't already gotten a call from Tom Parsons. Maybe this kind of news took a little while to filter through her organization to his. He remembered the time difference. CeCe's morning was three hours after his on the East Coast. And who knew what time she rolled into work each day. Probably late, knowing her.

None of that mattered. The roof might as well have just fallen in on him and the entire professional bull riding tour and it was all his fault.

"Aaron, I'm going to fix this."

It was sweet of her to offer but what did Jill think she could do? He let out a breath. "This is my mess. It's not yours to fix."

"Let me try. I've got an idea, but I need your help."

Garret came out into the hall and stopped when he saw

Aaron. No doubt, he looked like he'd just gotten some of the worst news he'd heard in a long time—which he had.

It felt like all the blood had drained out of his face. He could only imagine he looked as crappy as he felt right about now.

Aaron ignored that Garret was watching him and instead focused on Jill. "Uh, sure. Whatever you need."

"Do I remember correctly that Chase is in California?" she asked.

"Chase?" In the midst of possible career-ending news, Aaron felt the cold stab of jealousy cut through him when Jill asked about Chase. How crazy was that? "Um, I don't know." He glanced at Garret. "Is Chase in California?"

Garret nodded. "Yeah. He's visiting Leesa over the break. He flew out right after the competition."

"Yeah, he's there. Why?" Aaron relayed the information to Jill but still didn't know why she needed it. He sure would like to know though.

"I have an idea."

"Which is?" he asked. Why was she being so mysterious?

"I don't want to get your hopes up until I'm sure. Can you text me his cell number?"

"He's visiting his girlfriend." Aaron wanted that made very clear since Jill seemed so interested in Chase all of a sudden. And not even twenty-four hours after she'd been in Aaron's bed.

There had to be something else going on here. He could hope anyway.

"Okay, then give me her number. I just need to get in touch with him. We might be able to fix this mess with CeCe."

Aaron lifted his brows. Was Jill going to pimp Chase out to CeCe to make up for him disappointing her? Was that Jill's plan? "Um, Jill. You sure about this?"

"Trust me. I was with the company for two years. I picked up a few things while there. I really think I might be able to fix this. Aaron, let me try. Please."

"Okay." Feeling better that at least Jill wasn't looking to jump Chase for herself, he agreed. He still didn't know her plan, but he'd have to trust her to know what she was doing. "I'll text his number to you as soon as we hang up."

"Great. Thanks."

"Uh, Jill . . . are you doing okay?" Sad but true, he didn't want to hang up. He wanted to prolong the phone call and continue talking to her even if it would prevent her from moving on with her mysterious plan.

"I'll be better when I fix this."

"Can I ask you something?"

She sighed. "Sure."

He didn't miss the sound and he hated that he couldn't fix everything that was wrong himself. "Will whatever you're going to do get you your job back?"

She let out a short laugh. "No. Definitely not. In fact, if this works as I think it will, it will pretty much clinch it that I'll never work for CeCe Cole again."

"What? Then don't do it."

"I want to. And believe me, losing that job is not the end of the world. Working for CeCe was not all rainbows and unicorns."

After knowing the woman for just a few days, Aaron could believe that was true. "All right. I'll trust you to do what you think is right. Will you please keep me updated if anything happens? Good or bad."

"I will. I promise."

"Okay." He wanted to tell her he'd enjoyed their time together. He wanted to tell her he was sorry she'd gotten fired. Hell, he wanted to ask her if he could fly out there and help her. He didn't do any of that. Instead, he said, "I'll text you that number."

"Thanks. Bye."

"Bye." Glancing at Garret, Aaron lowered the phone. "That was Jill."

"That answers one of the dozen or so questions I still have about the call."

"Yeah, well, join the club." Aaron let out a snort. "You'd better sit down. I'll fill you in over a beer, or something harder. If you've got it, now might be a good time to break it out."

The largest sponsor of the pro bull-riding tour had just yanked all of her money. They were all gonna need a drink.

Aaron's phone buzzed. He leapt to look at it, hoping it was Jill. What he saw had him freezing all motion.

"Who is it?" Garret asked.

"Tom Parsons."

His friend widened his eyes. "You going to answer it?"

"No. That's for damn sure." Not moving, Aaron held the phone like it was a nuclear bomb at risk of detonating. When the call finally went to voice mail, he allowed himself to breathe again.

"What could he want?" Garret asked.

"To tell me CeCe just pulled all the sponsor money for the tour, most like." Aaron braced himself for Garret's reaction. It didn't disappoint.

Garret's eyes opened wider as his face seemed to lose color. "What are you going to do?"

"I guess I'll listen to that voicemail for starters." And avoid all calls from anyone affiliated with the association until . . . when? At least until he heard back from Jill, he supposed. Whenever that was.

What a fucked up mess.

CHAPTER TWENTY-SEVEN

The California sun shown brightly as Jill surveyed the scene, from the cars revving their engines, to the scurrying pit crews, to the crowd lined up along the track waiting for the race to begin.

It didn't take too long to spot the man she was looking for. He definitely cut an imposing figure. Besides that, he was in the VIP section reserved for owners and sponsors.

Jill moved toward the section. She flashed her old Cole Shock Absorbers all access pass, holding her breath until security waved her through. Once in, she made a beeline to her goal. "Mr. Cole?"

The older, slightly paunchy man turned at the sound of Jill saying his name. "Yes?"

"Hi, I'm Jill Malone. I used to work for you in the marketing department." His brow creased and he appeared to be thinking and trying to remember her. She helped him by adding. "When you still owned Cole Shock Absorbers."

"Oh, yeah." That information made him look far less happy to be speaking with her. "I suppose that means you now work for my ex-wife."

"No. We parted ways actually. The company just wasn't the same after you left." Jill smiled sweetly confident she hadn't told a lie. Just not the complete truth.

"Well, thank you, little lady. I miss the way things were myself."

"That's kind of what I wanted to talk to you about."

"You have news for me? My ex kick the bucket and forget to take me out of the will?" He let out a gruff laugh.

"Not exactly, but I do have some news that I'm not sure you're aware of." When he looked as if she had his attention, Jill continued, "I know how much you loved being involved with the professional bull riders. I dare say almost as much as you enjoy car racing."

"You're right about that. That bitch took that from me too."

"Well, maybe she's giving it back to you."

"What do you mean?"

"She ended the sponsorship."

"That no good, rotten . . ." John Cole continued with a string of obscenities that had a few people standing nearby staring and taking a step back.

"I think her mistake is your gain. There's a void that needs to be filled, Mr. Cole. And I think you're the perfect man to fill it."

"How you figure?"

"The auto parts division of the company, which you retain ownership of, has been floundering since the separation from the more well-known shock absorber division."

"Yeah. And?" He looked really unhappy that she knew that.

Jill rushed to make her point. "I think a high-profile sponsorship, a partnership with the bull-riding organization, is exactly what Cole Auto Parts needs. It will raise visibility and name recognition. And in addition to that, I think you should add a component that you've never explored before."

"What's that?"

"The bull riders themselves."

"The riders already wear the sponsor logos on their vests."

"I realize that, but these guys love nothing more than their vehicles. I think personal testimonials by the guys about how they only use Cole Parts in their trucks would go a long way to raise name recognition, brand value and ultimately sales. And these guys appeal to both men and women."

"Our target market ain't women, little lady."

Jill pushed down her feelings about his calling her *little lady*. "I know you believe that men are your only customers, but a lot of women are stuck bringing the family car in for service during the week while their husbands are at work. If they see a repair shop uses Cole Parts, a brand they're familiar with because their favorite rider personally recommends it as what he uses . . ."

He nodded. "I see where you're going."

"You know, I'm friends with Chase Reese. You might remember he was rookie of the year a couple of years back."

"Yeah, I remember."

"He's in town for a couple of weeks. I ran my idea by him the other night just to see what he thought of it, and he was excited about the opportunity to represent Cole Auto Parts. Says it's all he and his friends use. Actually, I invited him here for the race today." It was all planned right down to the second, but Jill feigned surprise. "Oh, look. There he is now. Right over there. Have you ever met him?"

John glanced in the direction Jill had looked and then back to her. "No, actually. I haven't."

"The guys are all really great. I got a chance to spend time with Chase last event. And Garret James and Aaron Jordan. Oh, and that adorable stock contractor Riley Davis, who took over her father's business after he died. Her and Skeeter Anderson are running it now. Skeeter was sweet enough to help her out."

John lifted his brows. "You seem to know quite a lot about the riders."

"Oh, yeah. They're really easy to be around. Such down-to-earth guys. Do you want to meet Chase? He's a natural in front of the camera. They really all are. That's what gave me the idea to use them in your ads to begin with." Jill tried to

act casual and pretend she was calm, but her heart thundered.
If this worked out, it would benefit both Mr. Cole's company and the organization . . . It had to work.

"All right. I wouldn't mind meeting him. But no promises about this idea of yours."

"Understood. Today isn't about business. Today is about racing." Jill smiled and turned to hale Chase while silently praying that Mr. Cole was just playing hardball.

Never letting his true feelings be known was the man's trademark. How he'd made it in business. She had planted the idea. She could only hope it would grow.

With Chase flashing his baby blues and pearly whites at the man, thereby proving he and the other guys would make the perfect spokesmen for Cole Auto Parts, he'd have to see the light.

If she could prove Cole Auto Parts would make the best sponsor for the bull riding organization, Mr. Cole would have no choice but to agree.

CHAPTER TWENTY-EIGHT

Sitting on the floor where he'd left it, Aaron's phone rang. The sound echoed off the block walls of Garret's garage.

Garret glanced down at him. "You going to get that?"

"Nope." Flat on his back on the weight bench, Aaron lifted the barbell off his chest and held it above his head before lowering it.

Spotting him from above, Garret nodded. "All right."

Aaron pushed the weight up again and held it there. "Take this. I'm done."

The call had distracted him and he'd lost count of his repetitions anyway. Garret lifted his brows but didn't say anything as he helped guide the bar to its resting place.

Aaron sat up and reached for the bottle of water on the floor. As he swallowed, he heard the alert for a new message.

He drew in a breath and let it out slowly. He didn't know who it was from but he could guess and figured he might as well see what this message was about.

He'd already listened to the voicemail where Tom Parsons had asked him what the hell had happened between him and CeCe, and the one where Tom had yelled about losing the sponsorship.

That call had ended with Tom's not-so-veiled threat that

said since Aaron had created this mess, he'd better figure out a way to fix it.

Going on day four of no contact from Jill, he'd given up hoping the call was from her. Whatever her plan was, it must not have worked. Now Aaron's main goal was to dodge any more calls from Tom. If he was smart, he'd stop retrieving the voicemails as well. It wasn't as if they were ever good news.

He hit the screen. When it lit he saw the missed call notification and let out a breath. "Crap."

"Parsons?" Garret asked.

"Yup." Aaron was ready to give up women altogether after this disaster. "He's probably calling to tell me they've voted to kick me out of the organization and that I shouldn't bother flying to California."

"Can they do that?" Garret asked.

"Hell if I know. Why couldn't they? It's a private organization. They can do whatever they want."

Aaron knew the news could be even worse than his getting kicked out. It could be Tom calling to tell them the organization had to cancel the rest of the season for lack of money. It wasn't cheap to run an event. To move the staff, equipment, and even the arena dirt, all over the country from week to week.

Ticket prices only covered a small portion. Without CeCe's money, their biggest sponsor, he didn't know how long the organization could continue to operate.

A glutton for punishment, Aaron hit to listen to the message. Whatever news was waiting for him, he'd rather know than not know so he could prepare himself.

"Jordan, I don't know how you pulled it off, but Cole Auto Parts just cut me a damned nice-sized check. We're all lucky they did too. I'll see you in California."

"That bad, huh?" Garret looked on with concern as Aaron remained shocked into silence.

"No. Not bad." He raised his gaze. "Cole Auto Parts just wrote the organization a big check."

175

Aaron wasn't sure what had happened or how to feel about it. He was relieved, but damn was he confused too.

Still in his hand, the phone rang again.

"Now what?" Garret asked.

This time, Aaron wasn't afraid to look at it. "It's Jill." Aaron said as he answered, "Hey, Jill. What's going on?"

She laughed. "I think something actually worked out, for once."

"I think you're right. The head of the organization just called to say he got a big check from Cole Auto Parts. What did you do?"

"I called in some favors with people I used to work with and found out John Cole was going to be at the races this weekend, then I made sure to be there with former Rookie of the Year Chase Reece to dangle in front of him."

"That's why you needed Chase's number." Realization crept in.

"Mmm hmm. I worked for Cole Industries long enough to know Mr. Cole loves bull riding. I think him losing the shock-absorber division upset him less than losing the big sponsor status. CeCe pulling the Cole Shocks sponsorship left the field wide open for him to step in and get a piece of what he lost back."

"Wow. Jill, you're brilliant." Brilliant and beautiful . . . and he wanted to see her again. "Are you coming to the event in California?"

"I don't know . . ."

"I'll leave a VIP pass under your name at the ticket window."

She hesitated. "When is it?"

"Friday night. You have to be there."

"Okay. I'll try to make it."

He didn't like she wouldn't commit to coming. "You have something else to do?"

It was none of his business. She wasn't his to question, but he couldn't help himself.

"As of now, no, but I hope to have something soon. I

started sending out resumés. I'm hoping they'll yield at least a couple of interviews. I might have to travel."

Aaron realized that although he was ready to celebrate because his problem was solved, hers wasn't. How could he have forgotten she still had no job? "I hope you get lots of calls."

"Thanks. Me too."

Selfish man that he was, he hoped those calls for job interviews came after the event. While he was hoping, he might as well wish for one more thing. That she'd land an incredible job closer to him. North Carolina would be perfect.

Aaron glanced at Garret, leaning against the wall and waiting for him to get off the phone. His presence was one thing that kept Aaron from spilling his guts and telling Jill he missed her. That he'd be willing to pay the airline fee and change his ticket to get out there sooner so he could spend time with her.

Instead, he said, "All right. So I guess maybe I'll see you at the arena."

"Maybe."

"Okay. Good luck with the job search."

"Thanks."

Out of small talk and unwilling and unable to say what he really wanted to, Aaron said, "So uh, goodbye for now."

"Bye, Aaron."

He disconnected the call and, still holding the phone in his hand, looked up to see Garret smiling. Aaron frowned. "What?"

"You've got it bad."

Aaron opened his mouth to protest, but instead he sighed. "Yup."

"What are you going to do about it?" Garret asked.

"Hell if I know."

"Okay. Moving on. You gonna fill me in on what she told you since I'm still pretty much in the dark here?"

"Yeah. Can we talk inside?" Fear for his future had ridden

Aaron for a week.

Now that it was gone, he realized how the constant worry had exhausted him. He needed to sit and regroup. Acclimate himself to the idea that he hadn't ruined his own career and taken down the whole organization at the same time.

Garret watched him for a moment before nodding and grabbing his own bottle of water off the ground. "Sure. We can be done here for today."

"Thanks."

"Besides, you'll be getting an extra hard workout this weekend in Cali. Sex is good for the core muscles." Garret patted his abs and grinned.

"Shut up." Aaron scowled, but damn if he didn't like that idea. It would be very nice if Garret's prediction proved correct.

CHAPTER TWENTY-NINE

"Do you see her yet?" Aaron strained to get a view of the VIP seating from where he stood.

"Who?"

When Aaron spun to his brother-in-law, he saw Garret was grinning. Aaron scowled. "Ha, ha. Very funny."

"I thought so." Garret continued to smile.

Annoyed, Aaron went back to concentrating on getting ready for the event.

He was working the rosin into his bull rope when Garret poked him and said, "Hey, Aaron."

Aaron didn't want to indulge Garret's little games, but he glanced up anyway. "Yeah?"

Garret tipped his chin to indicate something behind him. He turned and his heart kicked into a staccato in reaction to what he saw.

Jill was here. She wasn't in the chute seats. She was right down there on the floor behind the chutes on the same level Aaron was.

"Well, what are you waiting for? Go on over and say hello." It took Garret's prodding to spur Aaron into action.

"All right." Aaron abandoned what he'd been doing, leaving his rope hooked over the rail. He turned to go to Jill when he realized he still had his glove on. He tugged that off and looked for somewhere to leave it.

Rolling his eyes, Garret stepped forward. He grabbed the glove from Aaron. "Give that to me. Now go."

Aaron felt like a lovesick teenager, shaking as he walked fast toward Jill. When he got closer, he saw she wasn't alone. She was standing and talking to an older man.

Who the hell could that be?

"Hey." He touched her shoulder to get her attention. "Sorry to interrupt. I just wanted to say hello."

"No, I'm glad you did. Mr. Cole, this is Aaron Jordan."

"Nice to meet you, son."

Uh oh. This was CeCe's ex-husband. Aaron did his best to hide his surprise. "Uh, nice to meet you too, sir."

The surreal knowledge that Aaron had been with this man's ex-wife was enough of a burden. Then something CeCe had told him—about what her former husband had enjoyed in bed—flashed through Aaron's mind and the situation got even stranger.

"I've seen you ride. We just never had an opportunity to meet before this."

"I'm glad you got to meet now," Jill said to Mr. Cole. "Aaron's one of the riders I think would be perfect for the advertising campaign."

Advertising campaign? Jill sure had been busy.

Just when Aaron thought nothing else could surprise him, it seemed Jill had something else up her sleeve. "What campaign?"

"I didn't mention it because it's just an idea I had. It's up to Mr. Cole's marketing department whether they use it or not."

"Oh." Aaron nodded, still not having his answer but hoping to get it from her later. Hopefully in private. And naked.

He could only hope, because apparently while he'd been pining away, counting the days until this event when he might see her again, she'd been getting sponsorships and developing marketing plans and sending out resumés and who knew what else.

Not that he had wanted her to sit home miserable and missing him, but did she have to be quite so bubbly in her productivity? He felt a frown settle on his brow.

"I like your ideas, little lady. I think you might be the perfect addition to my marketing department."

Mr. Cole's words to Jill captured Aaron's attention, drawing him away from his internal whining. Aaron turned to see Jill's reaction. She looked flabbergasted.

"I don't know what to say." Jill's words surprised Aaron, as much as when she turned to him, as if looking for an answer.

He shrugged. "Say yes."

It was a job in her field and she wouldn't be working for CeCe. He didn't see the downside, except that if she took it she'd be staying in California—much too far away from him.

Mr. Cole laughed. "You should listen to him."

"I probably should. It's an amazing opportunity."

"But?" The older man waited for Jill to elaborate.

"I've been looking for a position on the East Coast so I can be closer to my family."

Which would also put her closer to Aaron. Shit. Now he wished he hadn't told her to take the job.

"Is that all that's holding you up?" John Cole waved one hand. "I've got offices in Charlotte you can work out of."

"Charlotte, North Carolina?" Aaron couldn't help but ask the question for her.

"Of course. The heart of the racing industry is there."

"Wow." Jill smiled. "In that case, I'd love to work for Cole Auto Parts. I can't thank you enough."

"No thanks necessary. Though I wouldn't mind you introducing me to that Riley Davis. I met her father a few years back. Good hardworking man and a great stock contractor. I'd love to meet the daughter who stepped into his footsteps."

Aaron lifted one hand to get the man's attention.

"Actually, I can arrange that. She's in back with the stock right now, but when she's done I'll bring her over to meet you."

After all the amazing things Jill had accomplished, Aaron was happy to contribute something.

"That would be fine." John had just agreed when Tom Parsons appeared.

He glanced between Aaron and John Cole. "Jordan. What are you doing here?"

Tom looked less than happy to find Aaron speaking with his new sponsor after the mess with CeCe.

"Just saying hello."

Still looking leery of Aaron standing even this close to his major benefactor, Tom turned to John Cole. "Let me show you to your seat, sir."

Apparently, Tom was taking over the sponsor babysitting duties personally. Good. If he'd done the same with CeCe, none of this would have ever happened.

Then again, had things been different, Aaron might not have met Jill.

After Tom had ushered Mr. Cole away, Aaron could fully concentrate on the real reason he was here. Jill.

"I'm glad you decided to come," he said.

She laughed. "So am I. I had no idea I'd come out of this event with a new job."

"A job in Charlotte." Barely an hour from where he lived. How perfect was that? At least, it would be perfect if Jill were interested in something more with him. Right now, Aaron was having trouble figuring that out. "I'm really happy for you, Jill."

"Thanks. I'm pretty happy too."

"So, you wanna go out and celebrate after?"

"Sure. I'd love to see all the guys and Riley."

"Or we could, you know, go alone. Grab something to eat. Maybe even order some champagne . . . in honor of your new job. My treat." When Aaron finally yanked his gaze up from where he'd been kicking the toe of his boot into the dirt, it was to see Jill smiling.

"You wouldn't mind skipping going out with the guys to take me out?"

"Mind? Hell, no. There's a lot I'd give just to spend time with you."

"Then, yeah, I'd love to go out with you after this is over."

Aaron couldn't help the smile that spread wide. "Good. We can talk about your plans. I can help you move, if you want. Even help you pack while I'm here. Help you look for a place in Charlotte too."

"That would be great."

"And if you need a place to stay in the meantime, I do have a spare room."

At his suggestive offer, there was a sly, sexy turning up of her lips. "Yes, you do."

"Of course, the mattress is kind of thin on the open-up sofa." He tipped his head to the side.

"Right. It is. Anywhere else I might be able to crash? Someplace nice and firm?"

Aaron laughed. "Yeah, I think I might be able to come up with something."

"You sure it wouldn't put a crimp in your social life having me hanging around your place? Get in the way of your going out. And you know, being with other girls," she asked.

Baffled how she could think he'd want anyone else when all he had thought about since dropping her at the airport had been her, Aaron shook his head and took a step closer. "Jill, you're the only girl I want."

"Really?"

"Really." He nodded.

Her smile lit her face. "Good."

Yeah. Things were very good.

Don't miss the rest of the Studs in Spurs novels for happy endings for all of your favorite heroes!

ABOUT THE AUTHOR

A top 10 *New York Times* bestseller, Cat Johnson writes the *USA Today* bestselling Hot SEALs series. Known for her creative marketing, Cat has sponsored bull riding cowboys, promoted romance using bologna and owns a collection of cowboy boots and camouflage for book signings.

For more visit CatJohnson.net
Join the mailing list at catjohnson.net/news